## "You've expected this ever since we met."

Logan continued quietly with a gleam in his eyes that Jennifer had never seen before. "I certainly wouldn't want to disappoint you." Then his lips covered hers, persuasively, demanding a response.

In horror she realized she was responding to him. Swiftly she turned her face away, tugging and pulling her arms free.

"Some man must have hurt you badly." Logan studied her grimly.

"No," Jennifer answered firmly, anger flashing in her eyes. "He didn't hurt me—my stupidity and ignorance did. I couldn't recognize a wolf when he was standing in front of me. I was blinded by charm and good looks."

"And now?" he asked.

"And now I can see through any disguise. I just hope my sister can," she answered sarcastically.

# JANET DAILEY AMERICANA

# DARLING
# JENNY

**Harlequin Books**

TORONTO • NEW YORK • LONDON
AMSTERDAM • PARIS • SYDNEY • HAMBURG
STOCKHOLM • ATHENS • TOKYO • MILAN

The state flower depicted on the cover of this book is
Indian paintbrush.

Janet Dailey Americana edition published June 1988
Second printing November 1988
Third printing November 1989
Fourth printing November 1990

ISBN 373-21950-4

Harlequin Presents edition published March 1978
Second printing May 1980
Third printing July 1981

Original hardcover edition published in 1974
by Mills & Boon Limited

Printed in U.S.A.

# CHAPTER ONE

'PLEASE fasten your seat belts,' the red light flashed above the arched doorway of the tourist section. Jennifer Glenn obeyed the instruction silently. She brushed back a strand of her red-gold, shoulder-length hair that had strayed to the corner of her eyes, tilting her head upwards towards the fresh, cooling air from the vent. As the breeze played lightly on her face, Jennifer's brown eyes were sadly contemplative.

She should have put her hair in its proper place, in a burnished bun on top of her head. Her mouth compressed painfully. Brad had liked it this way, loose and curling gently under her chin. Jennifer liked it this way, too, but it made her look so young and vulnerable. Just now she felt very old, much older than her meagre twenty-two years. But she had been vulnerable, so very vulnerable.

Just two short years ago she had graduated at the head of her class in secretarial school. Beaming and full of confidence, she had kissed her parents good-bye, climbed aboard the bus in Alexandria and headed for the big city—Minneapolis! For three weeks, she had made the rounds, in and out of executive offices, her certificates and recommendations proudly carried in her hand. And the results had always been the same.

She would walk into the room for her interview and see the impressed and interested looks on her interviewer's face change to one of doubt. After the second week, Jennifer could almost predict their reactions as they had studied her petal-smooth complexion, her bright, beaming eyes, her button nose sitting pertly in the middle of her face, and her red mouth that managed to spread into a wide nervous smile. Always the same unasked question had been in their faces—are you really twenty, you look more like sixteen. But instead they had murmured about her lack of experience.

Finally, the third week, with her reserves running short and the prospect of returning to the YWCA again that night without a job, Jennifer had practically pleaded with her interviewer to give her a chance to prove she was as good as her credentials said. With a fatherly look in his eyes, the man reluctantly had consented to place her in the attorney firm's typing pool. Jennifer could tell he had regretted his decision the minute he had made it, but at last she could write her anxious parents that she had a job.

For a year and a half she had stifled her naturally gregarious and exuberant personality so that she would appear efficient and businesslike even amid the gaggle of women. Secretarial positions in the attorney firm Smith, Katzenberg, Petersen, and Rohe, occupying fully two floors of a downtown office building, were few and far between. At last, after months of dull legal forms and hundreds of hours in front of a typewriter, Jennifer had got her chance. Mr. Bradley Stevenson's secretary had abruptly left her job, and a replacement was needed immediately.

The stewardess walked by, offering magazines to the plane's passengers. Jennifer declined politely when she stopped by her seat. She preferred to stare out of the plane's window at the misty fog of clouds that enshrouded it, her thoughts drawn back again. The memory was so very fresh. It might have been yesterday instead of six months ago.

Jennifer had known the minute she stepped into his office that things were going to change. After repeatedly being accused of lying about her age, she had begun wearing her hair piled on top of her head in an effort to appear sophisticated and older. She had known exactly what to expect of Bradley Stevenson. He had been termed one of the more brilliant young lawyers in the State and one of the most attractive bachelors in the firm. Although she had seen him several times in the building, this was the first time she had actually met him.

When she stepped into his office, a roguish lock of black hair had drifted over his forehead as he glanced up from his papers. The full force of his dark eyes settled on her, accompanied by a wide, extremely charming smile.

'Well, Miss Glenn,' he had said. 'You certainly have a very impressive record. Mrs. Johnston, your supervisor speaks very highly of you.'

There had been a few more pleasantries and questions about her qualifications, but Jennifer had known all along that the job was hers, that she was going to be the private secretary to this compelling, handsome attorney. The Minnesota farm girl had landed the most envied job in the firm.

With a stubborn determination born of self-will, Jennifer had set out to make herself indispensable to Mr. Bradley Stevenson. For three months she had sacrificed precious minutes of her lunch hour, stayed after hours typing crucial briefs, or seen that important correspondence was finished. In the beginning the extra effort was to prove that she was capable, but ever so gradually it was for the reward of his smile and brief words of appreciation. One particularly late night, he had insisted on taking her out to dinner despite her protests.

'I am your employer,' he had finally told her, 'and I demand that you accompany me to dinner.' Laughing, he had added, 'If it upsets your strict code of ethics to dine with your boss, pretend I'm going to give you some dictation over a glass of wine.'

'You really don't have to do this,' Jennifer had said, embarrassed at the growing colour in her cheeks and the pounding of her heart at the prospect of being with him in an informal atmosphere.

'If you have a date, say so. I certainly don't want to defend myself to a jealous lover.' His dark eyes had studied her intently as she had replied.

'Oh, I don't have a steady or anything like that. I don't go out very much.' Immediately she had regretted her words. To Jennifer, they had sounded too much like an invitation, so she had added brightly with a teasing glance, 'Besides, I've been working so hard.'

It had been a wonderful evening in a cosy, dimly lit

restaurant with Brad—he had insisted that she call him that—as he asked what seemed like really interested questions about her home life and background. That night when he had driven her to her apartment, and she had suitably thanked him for the evening, he had touched her arm and said,

'If you really enjoyed the evening, do me a favour. Tomorrow wear your hair down and have lunch with me, that is if I don't have another appointment. Do I?'

'No, you don't,' Jennifer had laughed gaily before getting out of the car and dashing happily into the building.

So it had begun. The occasional lunches and dinners had grown into dancing and theatres and hockey and football games until it had ended ... was it only two nights ago? .

'This is certainly the bumpiest ride I've ever had on a plane,' the lady seated next to Jennifer stated, bundling her knitting up and placing it in her tapestry bag. 'I've dropped three stitches in the last two minutes.'

Jennifer was suddenly conscious of the turbulent bouncing of the aircraft and murmured agreement with her seat companion. Taking Jennifer's polite comment as an invitation for conversation, the woman continued,

'I was in Salt Lake City with my daughter and her new baby. It's her first, and I told Richard, that's my husband, that it wasn't right for her to cope with those first few weeks on her own. Of course, it's our first grandchild and we were both dying to see her. Her name is Amy, a nice, old-fashioned name, I think.'

Jennifer nodded and smiled politely, wishing the

woman would stop talking and at the same time grateful to get her mind off that painful night.

'Are you going to Wyoming on a skiing holiday?' the woman asked. 'The weather's certainly perfect for it.'

'No. I'm going to stay with my sister for a while,' Jennifer answered.

'Oh, does she live in Jackson? I'm from outside Alpine myself. What does her husband do? Wouldn't it be a coincidence if I happened to know them? I know quite a few people there.'

'Sheila manages a motel in Jackson, but she's only been there a couple of years. Her husband was killed on active service with the army a few years ago,' Jennifer replied.

'Oh, that's too bad.' With a sudden movement, the woman turned towards Jennifer. 'Was it the Jefferies boy?' At the answering affirmative nod, she continued, 'I know his parents very well. It was such a trying time for them when he was listed as missing in action. They'd hoped for so long, only to learn he was dead.'

'Yes, it was quite a blow to them. That's why my sister moved to Jackson. She felt the children should get to know their grandparents better. And it would ease their grief, too.'

'You say she runs a motel. It's coming up on the busy time for her now with the holiday season just a few weeks away. Of course, the skiers are just a small few compared to the horde of tourists that descend on the Grand Teton and Yellowstone areas of Wyoming in the summer. Will your sister be waiting for you at

10

the airport?'

'Yes, I imagine so,' Jennifer replied.

'I hope she won't be too upset when we don't get there,' the woman stated.

'What do you mean?' Jennifer raised an arched eyebrow curiously.

'The weather, dear. Before I left Salt Lake, the radio said there were heavy snows in the Jackson Hole area,' the woman answered prophetically.

'Good afternoon. This is your captain speaking,' the pleasant, masculine voice said over the aircraft speaker system. 'I have some good news for you skiers. The temperature in Jackson Hole is thirty-two degrees. I've been told there's six inches of new powder on the slopes, and it's still coming down. Unfortunately, the wind is blowing and the visibility at the airport is below the required minimums for landing. That means we'll be landing at Idaho Falls instead. The airline will provide ground transportation for passengers to Jackson. You can check at the ticket counter when we arrive at Idaho Falls. Our arrival time will be twelve-fifty-five p.m. Thank you and happy skiing!'

Jennifer leaned back against her seat, turning her head towards the window to hide her misting eyes from the inquisitive woman at her side. She had been so looking forward to being with her sister again, especially after their brief telephone conversation the day before. Despite Sheila being five years older than Jennifer, they had always been close. A steady flow of letters from Jennifer had kept Sheila abreast of her sister's growing romance with Brad Stevenson. After that fateful night, Jennifer had turned to her sister rather than burden her parents with her heartbreak and humiliation. Jennifer's eyes cleared as she remembered with a smile Sheila's reaction to that last evening with Brad.

'Bradley Stevenson, brilliant, bold, and a brute,' Sheila had stated caustically, sympathetic anger lacing her words while recalling a favourite word game of theirs as youngsters. 'You certainly can't stay working for him. Going back to the farm and Mom and Dad isn't the answer. You need a complete change of scenery. Come and stay with me. I always get lonely at Christmas time for some of my own family. Besides, I can use the extra help you'd be at this time of the year when all the skiers descend on us. Catch the next plane out—and I won't take "no" for an answer. Besides, you've never seen snow until you've spent a winter in the Tetons.'

Happily and tearfully Jennifer had agreed.

'Write the folks a letter telling them your boss is sick and in the hospital or something and that you're taking leave of absence to come visit me,' Sheila had went on in her 'take charge' voice. 'Later on we can square it with them somehow.'

What a blessing it was to have a sister like Sheila, Jennifer thought, always so competent and understanding. Her sister had been the beautiful one of the family, with raven-black hair and unexpected blue eyes shining out from thick, dark lashes. Jennifer had been the 'cute' one, mostly because she looked like a perennial child.

'Please observe the "No Smoking" light and extinguish all cigarettes,' the stewardess's voice announced over the speaker. 'We've begun our final approach to Idaho Falls, and we'll be landing shortly. After landing, please remain in your seats until the plane has come to a full stop at the gates. Those passengers going to Jackson, Wyoming, are to report to the airline ticket counter. We are sorry for the inconvenience, and on behalf of the entire crew, we want to thank you for flying Western Airlines.'

Jennifer hugged the pale beige, suede coat around her as she hurried down the plane's steps into the building, amidst dancing snowflakes and a chilling wind. They should have been landing in Jackson right now, and she would have been rushing to meet her sister. Now she was faced with yet another journey and more time to think about what had happened and to feel sorry for herself.

Most of the other passengers had disembarked before Jennifer and were already huddled around either the ticket counter or the luggage area. She stood back in a less crowded area, waiting for the queues to thin out. Absently her fingers dug into the white sheepskin lining that spread on to the upturned collar of her coat as she gazed uninterestedly at the other passengers mumbling and beckoning impatiently at various clerks. She was suddenly looking into another pair of brown eyes that were interestedly inspecting her.

The unmasked appraisal in the man's glance was unsettling as Jennifer felt each curve and feature of her body inspected and weighed. She straightened her shoulders indignantly and scathingly surveyed him. She couldn't find much fault with what she saw. Even leaning back against a closed ticket counter, she could tell he was tall, over six foot, and the width of the brown suede Marlborough jacket across his shoulders couldn't be all sheepskin. The thumb of one hand was hooked in the waistband of his slacks, holding open the coat to reveal a white pullover over brown corduroy pants. There was a roguish look to his broad, strong face emphasized by the way his brown hair with its bronzed gold highlights was combed away from his forehead only to flip forward on one side in a wave. His eyes had a devilish and knowing gleam under thick curling lashes and gold-tipped brows. The crinkling lines at the corner of his eyes reminded Jennifer of her mother's 'perpetual laugh lines', as she preferred to call them. He had strong cheekbones and a good, chiselled nose. His lips had curled into a mocking smile by the time Jennifer noticed them, revealing a disconcerting dimple in his cheek.

Embarrassed that she had even deigned to return his stare, Jennifer looked away, skipping over his chin with the tiniest cleft in its centre. Colour and indignation rose within her as she quickly branded him lawless, lordly, and a Lothario. And she'd had all the exposure to the latter that she wanted!

The line had thinned out at the luggage centre, and Jennifer quickly stepped towards it and away from the stranger. She was just reaching down to pick up one of her bags when a low baritone voice said, 'May I help you?' Then an arm reached passed her and picked up

14

her case.

She straightened to glare angrily into the mocking eyes of the stranger she had seen only a few seconds before.

'I can manage perfectly,' Jennifer replied frostily, reaching for her bag.

'You are Jennifer Glenn, aren't you?' he stated with a horrible, knowing smile. 'I didn't see any other redheads get off the plane.'

'My hair isn't red. It's strawberry blonde,' Jennifer asserted.

'Sheila called my hotel and told me your plane was being re-routed here. Is that yours, too?' He was reaching down for a blue suitcase that matched the one in his hand.

'Yes,' Jennifer answered, momentarily surprised at her sister's name. 'Who are you?'

'I'm sure Sheila's mentioned me in her letters. The name is Taylor, Logan Taylor.'

'So the "L" was right after all. Lawless, lordly, and a Lothario,' Jennifer thought with a triumphant gleam in her eye.

His hand had taken her elbow, and he was guiding her through the crowd. Sheila had mentioned him in her letters, but Jennifer had always received the impression that he was much older. He wasn't over—she glanced at his face from the corner of her eye—thirty-one, thirty-two? He owned the motel that Sheila managed, and plenty else, from what her sister had intimated in her letters.

'I thought you might like a cup of coffee and relax

a little before we leave,' Logan Taylor was saying as he ushered Jennifer into the café area.

'Leave? Leave for where?'

'Jackson Hole, of course.' He pulled out a chair at one of the tables for Jennifer before seating himself.

'But the airline . . .'

'I already let them know that I was meeting you. Luckily your sister caught me just as I was checking out of my hotel. She knew I was driving back today. Since you'll be staying with her, the ride will give us a chance to get better acquainted.' His drifting glance once more swept over her face in appraisal. 'What will you have? Coffee?'

'Yes, that's fine. Black, please,' she ordered as the waitress approached their table. Jennifer waited until the girl had moved away before she replied a little icily to his previous statement and his glance. 'I doubt if we'll see very much of each other, Mr. Taylor.'

'It's Logan, and Jackson Hole isn't that big. We'll see each other.' He leaned back against his chair as the young waitress brought their coffee and set it in front of them on the table. He smiled up at the girl warmly, but only Jennifer saw the waitress blush under his glance. Sickening was her immediate reaction, and it must have shown on her face because Logan Taylor glanced at her with a puzzled expression.

'Logan!' a feminine voice cried. 'Logan! So you didn't leave after all!'

Jennifer looked up just as a pair of the most ravishing girls descended on their table. A blonde who was wearing a fur coat that looked as if it would have cost a

16

year of Jennifer's salary.

'I came to pick up Rachel, and I find you. If only you'd told me this morning, we could have come out together,' she pouted as she glanced over her shoulder at the long-haired brunette who was staring seductively at Logan. 'Isn't it the greatest thing, Rachel? Here I was bemoaning the fact that Logan had left, and I find him here at the airport. I should have known you would change your mind about driving back in this weather, especially after the late night we had.'

Jennifer nearly sighed in disgust at the blatant way they were throwing themselves at him. And he was standing there taking it as if it was his due.

'Who's the little girl, Logan?' Rachel asked huskily, her dark eyes never leaving Logan's face.

'This is Sheila Jeffries' sister, Jennifer. DeeDee Hunter and Rachel Scott,' Logan introduced as Jennifer sat in fuming silence.

'It's only the second week of December. I didn't know school vacation started so early,' the blonde DeeDee said.

'Twenty-two years old hardly qualifies me as school age,' Jennifer retorted sharply.

'Are you really that old? You look much younger.' DeeDee answered in disbelief as Jennifer met the teasing glance of Logan's brown eyes. But the blonde's interest in Jennifer didn't last long before DeeDee turned her rapt face back to the man beside her. 'We're having a welcome home party for Rachel. You must come tonight.'

'I'm driving back to Jackson Hole this afternoon,'

17

Logan stated quietly, ignoring the petulant expression on the blonde's face. 'I stayed just long enough to pick up Jennifer. We'll be leaving in a few minutes. Next time, maybe.'

'Keep them hanging on the string,' Jennifer thought disgustedly.

'You really shouldn't drive in this weather,' Rachel protested. 'Why don't you stay until it lets up?'

'No, I'm sorry,' he said firmly.

'You are mean, Logan Taylor,' DeeDee pouted. 'But don't you forget to make reservations for us. A party of eight, the weekend after Christmas.'

'I won't forget,' Logan nodded.

'We'd better dash. See you soon, darling,' DeeDee smiled, disentangling herself from his arm, then blowing him a kiss as she began to push Rachel towards the door. 'Nice meeting you, Janet.'

'You too, DoDo,' Jennifer mumbled.

'What was that you said?' Logan asked, seating himself once again in the chair beside her.

'Nothing. Listen, if I'm keeping you from something, I'm sure I can still catch the airline's transport.' Jennifer sipped at her coffee, before pushing a strand of her copper-gold hair behind her ear.

Strong fingers captured her chin and turned it towards him. Quickly she jerked herself away, her heart hammering in her throat.

'I thought for a minute your eyes were green,' he mocked, picking up his coffee and raising the cup to his mouth. His eyes twinkled over at her. 'They're still brown.'

Jennifer rose angrily from the table. 'If you're ready to go, I'd like to leave now and get this trip over with.'

'For someone who's not a redhead, you certainly have a short temper!' Logan laughed.

## CHAPTER TWO

SNOWFLAKES fell with a blurring density around the four-wheel drive vehicle obscuring Jennifer's vision until she seemed adrift in a grey-white cloud. The only other occupant in her snow-surrounded world was the last person she would have chosen, the man behind the wheel, Logan Taylor. She glanced over at his profile, his attention concentrated on the few feet visible in front of them. The needle hovered at the thirty mark on the speedometer.

'Well, Jenny Glenn, are you going to maintain this silence for another two hours?' His hand flexed tensely on the steering wheel as he scowled out at the heavy snow mist.

'My name is Jennifer,' she corrected, her mouth setting itself in a firm little line as she spoke.

'I like Jenny Glenn better. It rolls so easily out of your mouth and forces you to smile. Jenny Glenn.' The dimple appeared once again as he repeated her name, glancing over at her with a disturbing twinkle in his eyes.

'I hate the name, Jenny,' Jennifer protested, even though the way he said it, it sounded rather nice. 'It sounds like a donkey or a mule!'

He glanced at her again. This time his smile was

wide and unmistakably teasing. There was so much fun and warmth in his gaze that Jennifer had to look away or be drawn by his magnetic charm. She shivered slightly as she wondered if she was going to be the kind of woman who was always susceptible to the Casanovas of this world.

'Are you cold? There's a blanket in the back if you want to cover your legs,' Logan offered, his swift gaze taking in the nylon-covered legs beneath her olive skirt.

'No, I'm fine. Just a ghost walking over my grave, I guess,' Jennifer shrugged. She stared out at the smoky gauze of snowflakes. 'Do we have much farther to go?'

'Twenty—thirty miles, I imagine.'

'I hope Sheila isn't worried about me,' Jennifer mused.

'She won't be. You're with me,' Logan asserted. The devilish gleam in his eye mocked her.

'And that makes everything all right, doesn't it?' she retorted sarcastically.

Logan Taylor didn't reply as he slowed to negotiate a curve in the road. The snow had begun to drift, covering the highway until it was difficult to see it. But the reflector poles on the side of the road formed an imaginary corridor of safety. The jingling of chains added another touch of reassurance.

'You don't like me very much, do you?' Logan commented, his eyes never leaving the road as a cross-wind tugged at the jeep.

'Don't be ridiculous. I hardly even know you,'

Jennifer lied.

'Who's being ridiculous? I think you've already got me all judged and sentenced. Don't I fit the picture that Sheila described?'

Jennifer glanced at him coolly, taking in the brown of his hair, the bronze highlights hidden in the dimness, and the strong, chiselled jawline. Only masculine adjectives sprang to her mind, powerful, virile, arrogant, and no doubt, very experienced in the art of love.

'No, my impression was of someone older, more settled, a family person,' she replied honestly with a hint of rebuke in her voice. 'How long has my sister known you?'

He laughed lightly.

'Quite a while. Eric was my best friend. As a matter of fact, we both met Sheila at the same time. Your sister is a very beautiful woman. We both tried to date her, but Eric won. I couldn't make it to the wedding, or I probably would have met you. When Sheila moved out here, I naturally made a point of seeing her and the children. Little Eric is quite a man despite his seven years and Cindy tries very hard to emulate him.'

'You must see them quite often,' Jennifer commented, wondering if his interest was in the children of his best friend or her sister who had once spurned him in favour of another.

'I do. Your sister has a very admirable sense of independence, but once in a while she finds it convenient to have a man around to lean on. Paul and Katie, Eric's parents, have a tendency to spoil the children, which is only natural for grandparents, so I step in occasionally as a father figure to them. I serve as a steadying influence on them and keep them from demanding too much from Sheila.'

'You're a regular "big brother",' Jennifer commented sarcastically.

'What's that supposed to mean?' he asked with ominous quietness.

'That's what you are, aren't you? With your—er—anxious regard for my sister and her family,' she retorted, her eyes widening in false innocence.

'How long has it been since you visited her?' His eyes narrowed as he glanced at her.

'I saw her when she was home this past spring, but if you're referring to coming out here, this is the first time.'

Jennifer tossed her red-gold hair out of her eyes with a defiant movement of her head.

'You haven't seen her spend an afternoon with the children, and then work till all hours of the night on the things that she should have done during that time. Or the way she looks wistfully at her sketchbook and dreams of the ideas in her head being put on canvas. You haven't seen Eric and Cindy vying for her undivided attention during the precious moments they're together. Or the way they act so adult so they won't be a burden to her. It wouldn't matter if I'd never known her husband, I would still be interested in doing everything I could to help her. Now, you can turn up your nose and call me "big brother", but it isn't going to stop me.'

Jennifer flinched under the piercing censure of his

glance. She had meant to provoke him, to show her dislike and disdain for his interest in her sister. But she had disturbed the still waters of his easy-going outwardness and revealed the hidden and possibly treacherous depths of his indomitable character.

'I should have known it was impossible for there to be a second person as selfless and sincere as Sheila,' Logan muttered.

Jennifer realized she had asked for that put-down. At least now she knew just how much of a help she could be to Sheila, and not just an extra piece of baggage on an already heavy load.

The jeep fishtailed slightly as she started to apologize. One look at Logan's face was enough to tell her that now wasn't the time for talking. The few feet of road visible in front of them was a glaze of ice. Then ahead of them, the road began to curve.

'Hold on, Jenny. I don't think I'm going to make this turn.'

Silently, intently, she could almost feel him will the jeep around the corner. For an instant it looked as if he was going to make it, then a spray of snow flew on to the windshield as they careered off the road. They bumped and bounced to a halt, the snow on the windshield being slashed away by the pulsating beat of the wipers until again the smoky white world outside could be seen.

'Jenny? Jenny, are you all right?' Logan's hand was brushing the hair away from her face while his eyes examined her intently.

'I'm f-f-fine,' she managed in a shaky voice. With a

nervous laugh, she added, 'I was scared out of my wits, though.'

'So was I,' he smiled. 'Nothing's broken? You didn't hit anything?'

'No,' she reassured him with a smile. His anxious and rather solicitous regard made her feel warm and safe inside, and she was sorry when he moved away.

'Well then, I'd better see what we've got ourselves into.'

He opened the door to a storm of snow and biting cold winds. His form was strangely dark in the obscure white void as he moved first to the front, then disappeared to the rear of the jeep. Seconds later he was back inside with snowflakes covering his head and coat, and his breath made smoky puffs in the cold.

The audacious twinkle was back in his eyes as he met her serious gaze. 'I have some good news and some bad news. Which would you like first?'

'Give me the good news first,' Jennifer smiled.

'We're stuck.'

'Good heavens, what's the bad news?' she asked in a note of alarm.

'There's a building a few hundred feet back up the road with smoke coming out of the chimney,' Logan grinned.

For a brief moment, anger rose inside her before her innate sense of humour took over, and she burst into laughter.

'At last I know you have a sense of humour.' His laughter finished into a satisfied smile. 'It would have been rough throwing ourselves into a strange house if we were still at each other's throats.' His gloved hand patted the steering wheel thoughtfully. 'Well, you'd better bundle up. It's going to seem like a long hike in this weather.'

Jennifer nodded and pulled the hood of her suede coat over her head, fastening it securely around her neck. Taking her fleece-lined gloves out of her pocket, she swiftly slipped them on to her hands, glancing over at Logan as she finished.

'Get out my side. The snow's tramped down a bit more.'

She slid behind the wheel as he got out of the jeep. Logan was standing calf-deep in snow beside the door as she swung her legs around to get out.

'Those boots are going to do you about as much good as a dustpan when you're trying to shovel through a ten-foot snowdrift,' he laughed as he looked at her petite, fur-trimmed snowboots.

'I think they're only good for cleared walks and ploughed streets,' Jennifer agreed ruefully, too fully aware of how much bare leg was going to be in the snow just standing where Logan was now.

He slid an arm under her knees. 'Put your arm around my neck. I'll carry you to the road,' he instructed, as his other arm encircled her back and waist.

For a second, Jennifer wanted to protest. She didn't want to be in such close contact with this man, but the foolishness of such a protest prevented her. After all, it was the most practical thing to do. So she relented, her arms encircling his neck.

They were only twenty feet from the road, but the

wind was blowing directly into them. Jennifer was glad that she could hide her face in the brown suede of his coat, not just to protect her face from the icy blasts of the wind, but also to keep Logan from seeing the rising colour in her cheeks. Then he was placing her on her feet, retaining a hold on one hand while huddling down towards her in the flurry of snowflakes and wind.

'We'll walk now,' he nearly shouted, as the wind tried to whip his voice away. 'Keep a hold of my hand so I don't lose you in a snowdrift.'

They struggled against the upsurging cold blasts while the falling and blowing flakes danced maliciously around them. The fallen snow tugged at their feet, pulling and dragging to slow their pace. Then Logan stopped.

'We'll cut across here.' He pointed across the snow to the shadowy grey outline of a building. 'The snow may be deep. I can carry you.'

'No, no,' Jennifer protested. 'It's too far. If you go ahead of me and break the path, I'll be okay.'

His dimples were two dark clefts in his cheeks as he grinned at her, but didn't argue. He stepped into the untouched snow, his legs moving in close, scissor-like motions to leave behind a white furrow for her to walk in. The wind pushed at her as she tried to concentrate on staying in the narrow lane, steeling her numbing legs against the flurry of cold snow kicked up by Logan's feet. She felt like a tightrope walker balancing on the high wire.

It felt as if they had covered miles as Jennifer glanced around Logan's shoulder to see the house still some distance ahead of them. She was out of breath and the numbing cold grabbed at her legs, making her steps awkward and clumsy. Then she stumbled, falling on her knees into the snow.

'I'm so cold,' she panted as Logan pulled her out of the snow and brushed away at the snow clinging to her skirt and legs. 'I can hardly catch my breath.'

'It's the altitude,' he muttered with an expression of self-disgust. 'We're probably around seven thousand feet.'

Without asking permission, he swept her up into his arms. Jennifer had no strength to refuse. She was just grateful to hold exhaustedly on to his shoulder, as he carried her to the house.

She was disappointed when they were finally close enough for the snow to cease obscuring their vision. It was just a log cabin, not a house, a forlorn little building sitting isolated amidst the trees that poked their white-covered heads over the roof. She glanced at Logan's face to see his reaction, but there was none. They had barely reached the doorstep when the door swung open.

Standing in the opening was a lean, gaunt old man, his face covered by a growth of greyish-white hair with matching strands sticking out from the cap on his head. His shoulders were stooped and bent beneath the red flannel shirt he wore. As Logan stepped closer, Jennifer saw that the youthful flames in the old man's dark eyes denied that the fires of life were even thinking of dying. There was anything but welcome in his expression as he glared out at them.

'What in tarnation do you want?' he fairly roared at Logan.

'My jeep got stuck in the snow out by the road,' Logan replied easily, ignoring the hostility that had greeted him. 'I noticed the smoke coming out of your chimney, and I thought we might impose on you for some shelter tonight.'

'You're a pair of damn fools to be out in weather like this!' He grudgingly opened the door wider and stepped to one side so they could enter. 'Might as well come in before she freezes to death in that get-up.'

Logan thanked him sincerely as he stepped through the door and set Jennifer on her feet. His eyes twinkled merrily as he saw the apprehensive expression on her face.

'Ain't much, ain't got nothin' much, but you're welcome to stay.' The backhanded invitation was given in a growly and irritated voice.

When Jennifer's eyes adjusted from the light outside to the dimness of the cabin, her first reaction was, this is it, one room, four walls, that's all! Then the immaculate cleanness struck her. The wood floors reflected the flames burning in the fireplace across the room and the little table sitting in the middle was covered with a bright red checked cloth. On the wall to the right of the fireplace was a sparkling white porcelain monstrosity, its chrome handles shining from the light of the fire. Even the black circles on top seemed to glow from hand-rubbed care. It was a stove, one of those huge, wood-burning stoves. The wood cabinets, on the wall where the door was, gleamed with care. The bed on the left had a brightly coloured quilt thrown over it.

'Want some help with your boots, Jenny?' Logan offered, his voice tearing her attention away from the cosy room.

'No, thank you,' she shook her head, bending down to her task as Logan turned back to their host.

'The name is Logan Taylor. I own the Box T spread on the south Gros Ventre Range. This is Jenny Glenn. We really appreciate you taking us in like this.'

'Taylor, you say? Seems like I know your old man. Used to be a fair hunter, didn't he?' the man commented, inspecting Logan closely. 'I don't hold with huntin' for pleasure. They oughta make people eat what they kill.'

'My father passed away several years ago, but he used to hunt quite a lot,' Logan agreed, shedding his coat. 'He always said there was nothing quite as good as a juicy venison steak.'

'Humph!' the old man snorted. 'S'pose that's an invitation to eat with me. Get yourselves over by the fire, and I'll go carve us up some steaks. Name's Carmichael,' he stated, thrusting a gnarled hand reluctantly towards Logan. 'She cook?' At the amused expression on Logan's face as he glanced towards Jennifer, the man shuffled over to the rack beside the door where his coat hung. 'Only two things I can't abide,' he said, 'a woman that can cook and one that can't.'

Logan walked over to the fire and extended his hands to the flames as Jennifer joined him. He smiled down at her reassuringly.

'He's quite a cantankerous old man, isn't he?' he said, glancing down at the shimmering copper highlights in her hair. She nodded agreement as he turned back to the fire. 'You'll want to change into some warmer clothes. I'll go back and get your cases.'

'You really don't need to,' Jennifer protested. 'I can get by in what I'm wearing.'

'Nonsense,' Logan retorted firmly. He stepped away from the fireplace to draw up a cane-backed rocker. Taking Jennifer's hand, he led her to the chair and sat her down. 'You wait here. I'll only be gone a minute.'

'At least wait until you've warmed up some more.'

'No. It's almost dusk now. If I wait any longer I'll be fumbling around in the dark.'

Jennifer watched reluctantly as he buttoned up his coat and pulled on his gloves. With a cheery salute, he opened the door and went outside.

He was being awfully kind, Jennifer thought, leaning back in the rocker to rest her feet on the hearth and wriggle her toes in the warmth from the fire. Of course, that was his nature, to be charming. Still, he could be a lot of fun just as long as you didn't take him too seriously. But what about Sheila? At this point in time, she probably would be terribly susceptible to Logan's type of man. And men like him had an uncanny knack of appearing to be what a woman wanted most in a man. Luckily, Brad Stevenson had taught Jennifer that lesson. Now she could look at Logan and see the amber caution light flashing its 'beware' sign.

A whoosh of snow and wind announced the return of the grizzled old man as he stomped in through the door. He dropped his loosely wrapped package on the counter with a thud, ignoring Jennifer's smile of welcome.

'Would you like me to help you with something?' she offered as he busied himself at the old range.

'Nope, can't stand women in my kitchen.'

At that moment Logan came hurrying in the door.

'Brrr! I think it's getting worse out there,' he shuddered, knocking the snow off his trousers and boots as he set the cases down before walking over to warm himself by the fireplace.

'Most likely is,' the old man remarked. 'One thing about Wyoming weather in the winter—you can be sure it's going to be one of three things: It's gonna snow until you swear the mountains got a bad case of dandruff; or it's gonna be colder than your wife's feet on a winter night, or the wind's gonna blow until your teeth chatter right out of your mouth. It's really hell when it does all three!'

The rich, deep chuckle from Logan brought Jennifer's laughing eyes around to him.

'Mr. Carmichael is right. You don't know what winter is until you've spent it in the Tetons, Jenny,' Logan smiled down at her warmly. 'Is there a place for her to change clothes?'

'There's the privy. That door there on the left of the fireplace.' The old man nodded his head at the fireplace. 'Promised Margaret forty years ago I'd get her indoor plumbing, but she up and died before I got it all put in. Those frozen pipes are a damned nuisance.'

It was an extremely small room, as Jennifer found

out. The large, four-legged, cast-iron bathtub took up most of the room, leaving her only about two feet of clear space for manoeuvring. But she finally succeeded in getting the olive green slacks and sweater on without seriously banging herself into the wall.

Later Jennifer was inspecting the wide selection of books in the makeshift bookcase sitting in the far corner of the cabin as Mr. Carmichael bustled around setting the table by the light of a hurricane lamp.

'Haven't you ever considered hooking up to electricity?' Logan asked. 'It runs right outside your cabin by the road.'

'Too expensive,' the old man snorted ruefully. 'Besides, what do I need it for?'

'You certainly have a wide variety of books,' Jennifer interrupted, picking up a worn copy of Mark Twain's *Tom Sawyer* nestled snugly between Shakespeare's *Romeo and Juliet* and Dickens' *Oliver Twist*.

'Didn't ya think I could read?' he grumbled, shuffling over to the fireplace to fish out the potatoes from the coals.

'Oh, that's not it at all,' Jennifer apologized quickly. 'I just thought. . . .'

'I know, that a crotchety old buzzard like me wouldn't be readin' that kind of stuff,' he growled. 'Well, sometimes I even read the labels off my tin cans. Come on over and sit down. Supper's on the table.'

The meal, for all its simplicity, was delicious. The steaks were tender and juicy, and Mr. Carmichael informed Jennifer that it was elk and not deer venison. There were thick slices of sourdough bread toasted so the good nutty flavour came through, baked potatoes, stewed tomatoes that had a very savoury blend of seasonings, and to finish the meal a steaming cup of the blackest coffee Jennifer had ever seen. She sipped the bitter brew hesitantly and watched in astonishment as Logan and Mr. Carmichael drank it calmly.

'Coffee's kinda weak,' the old man grumbled. 'It's really good when you can slice it with a knife.' Then he guffawed loudly at the startled expression on Jennifer's face as he winked gleefully at Logan. 'This here's "man's coffee". It'll put hair on your chest. None of that tea-lookin' stuff you women fix.' Turning to Logan, the old man's eyes burned fiery bright as he added in a more serious tone, 'That's a right purty woman. I knowed many a woman in my younger days. She's gonna be one of those that always look like a child. Her skin ain't gonna be crinklin' up into a prune face.' He glanced back at Jennifer as if to reassure himself of his opinion, then returned his gaze to Logan. 'Noticed earlier, too, she's got a fine pair of hips, wide and strong. Oughta have some healthy babies.'

Jennifer's mouth opened in astonishment at his presumptuous statement, only to close it quickly as she met the mocking gleam in Logan's eyes.

'Let me do the washing up, Mr. Carmichael,' she offered, hoping to get off this embarrassing turn of conversation and hide the growing colour in her face.

'Nope, I'll do 'em,' he denied quickly, as he pushed his chair away from the table. 'Course, if you want to make yourself useful, you can get them old quilts out of the trunk and make up a bed on the floor beside the fireplace.'

Anything just to get away from those teasing brown eyes, Jennifer thought, sending Logan a withering glance. The trunk was sitting at the foot of the bed, which was really little more than a cot. A wave of fatigue swept over her as she looked longingly at the quilted bedcover. It was—what—eight o'clock? she wondered. But she was certainly tired. She lifted the heavy wooden lid of the trunk and tilted it back until it rested against the bed.

There was one extra thick quilt that Jennifer decided she could use to cushion the wood floor. The other two lighter weight quilts could be used for covers. A little smile flitted across her face as she pictured with amusement Logan crawling under the covers with their grizzled host. Minutes later she had the blankets spread on the floor, the top two covers turned back invitingly.

'I couldn't find any pillows, Mr. Carmichael,' she said, turning towards the counter where he was putting the last of the dishes in the cupboard.

Grunting with seeming displeasure, he shuffled over to the highboy dresser, pulled open one of the lower drawers, and removed two square satin pillows. He walked over and handed them to Jennifer with a gruff, 'Use these.'

Needlepointed on the front of one was a charming picture of a log cabin with blue smoke rising from the chimney and the words 'Home Sweet Home' beneath it. But it was the other one that really caught Jennifer's eyes—a large red heart with lace edges covered the front with 'My Darling' scrolled inside. She choked with laughter as she wondered mischievously which one of their heads was going to rest on it. Without a word she placed them side by side on top of the quilts.

Finished, she curled up in the rocker by the hearth and stared into the hypnotic flames. She glanced over at Logan, but he was watching the old man at the counter with the most peculiar, calculating expression on his face.

'Well, dishes are all done,' Carmichael announced, his shuffling feet taking him over to the cot. 'If you folks don't mind, I'll go ahead and turn in. You're welcome to go to bed whenever you've a mind to.'

Jennifer sat in horrified silence, barely hearing Logan speak up quickly.

'I was wondering if it would be all right for Jenny to sleep in your bed tonight.'

'In my bed?' their host exclaimed incredulously, his gnarled fingers digging into the mattress as if he thought they were going to steal it from beneath him. 'What's wrong with the one she made ya on the floor?'

Jennifer stared from Logan to Mr. Carmichael to the quilts on the floor. Hysteria welled up inside her. It was a dream! A nightmare! It couldn't be true!

Suddenly it wasn't an old brick fireplace she was in front of, it was a sparkling white one. The quilts on the floor became a plush fur rug, and she was lying on it in the arms of Brad Stevenson. She was kissing him ... no, she was fighting him, pushing off the hands that were trying to slip under her sweater, twisting, struggling to free herself from his embrace until at last

36

she had wrenched herself away. Brad was shouting at her.

'Don't pull that innocent, hard-to-get act with me!' he was saying, his lips curling in anger. 'You knew exactly what was going to happen when I invited you here. That baby-face of yours won't cut any ice now. I've been coming across with the dough and fine manners for weeks now. And you! You're going to come across tonight!'

She remembered looking down at him, filled with disgust that she had actually wanted to fall in love with this man. This wolf! Then she had run. Run, until she had come full circle back into almost the same situation.

'That's my bed!' The old man was saying. 'It's got my lumps in it. You two are young. Your bones aren't brittle like mine. A night sleepin' on the floor ain't gonna hurt her.'

'But you don't understand,' Jennifer whispered in a strained voice. 'We aren't married.'

'Ya will be. I seen the way you two have been lookin' at each other.' He glanced at Logan with a conspiratorial smile before adding belligerently, 'Because it's my house and I say I'm sleepin' in my bed!.'

# CHAPTER THREE

LOGAN rose from his chair by the table to walk over by the fire. Tears misted Jennifer's eyes as she looked pleadingly at Logan. When he refused to return her glance and continued to stare sombrely into the flames, she rose to stand by his side.

'Please,' she whispered, touching his arm lightly, 'you've got to do something.'

He studied her face, the anxious, almost fearful expression in her eyes. He shook his head in puzzlement.

'I don't know what we can do,' he said, flashing a swift glance behind him at the man sitting on the bed.

'I can't possibly sleep in the same bed with you!' Nothing masked her horror mixed with embarrassment. She stared at the stark whiteness of the sweater covering his chest.

'Don't get hysterical about it,' Logan said, calmly and softly. 'Let's look at this sensibly. We're both fully clothed and there's nothing that says we can't go to bed in what we've got on. Not only that, I can sleep on the side here by the fire and just use the one cover. You can sleep on the other side under both covers.'

Jennifer hugged her arms about her. It was logical.

It wasn't as if they had any real choice.

'He's an old man, Jenny,' Logan continued, 'and it's not as if I were going to try to rape you. After all, there's a witness,' he finished with an accusing gleam of mischief in his eyes.

She studied his face intently. Except for the dimple in his cheek, he seemed sincere enough. The whole question was could she trust him, believing with certainty, as she did, that when he had previously shared his bed with a woman, it had not been for sleep?

'Okay,' she gave in grimly. 'But stop calling me Jenny. And so help me, if you . . .'

'Don't worry,' he grinned, holding up his hand in a mock promise. 'I swear I won't lay a hand on you.'

'You'd better not or I'll scream so loud there'll be an avalanche,' Jennifer said firmly.

'Go on. You're exhausted. You might as well crawl under the covers and get some rest.' Logan pushed her lightly towards the quilts. 'I'm going to have a cigarette and relax.'

Jennifer didn't argue with that. Although as she slipped under the covers, she glanced at him distrustfully. Then she noticed the bright red pillow at her head. Quickly she reached and exchanged it for the one closer to the fireplace.

'Good night, Jenny Glenn,' Logan laughed, amused by her defiant gesture.

'Good night,' Jennifer replied in a hard, decisive voice.

She turned away from the fire to the darkness of the cabin. The silence of the room touched her until the night sounds took over, the slow stirrings of their host in his cot, the slight creaking of the rocker where Logan sat, and the crackling and popping of the fire. The loudest of all was the howling of the wind outside as it shook and rattled at the door until Jennifer felt like one of the little pigs with the wolf outside huffing and puffing to blow the house in.

As tired as she was, sleep escaped her. The hardness of the floor under the heavy quilt pushed at her bones while the pillow felt like a lumpy rock under her head. She felt as if she was waiting for something to happen, for Logan to crawl under the covers with her. Her muscles tensed as she heard him rise from his chair. She listened to the ominous clunk of his boots hitting the floor. Then there was the muffled sound of his stocking feet as he walked towards her. She closed her eyes quickly. He was lifting the top cover and ... that was all! Just the top cover as he had promised!

She listened to his even breathing while hers was held in apprehensively. But he just laid there on his back.

'Go to sleep, Jenny,' he whispered softly. 'Everything's going to be all right.'

As if on command her muscles relaxed and she drifted off to sleep, feeling strangely safe and secure.


'You certainly are bright-eyed this morning,' Logan chided, studying her rapt face with interest.

'I can't believe how beautiful it is out here,' Jennifer murmured, gazing around her at the white wonderland of snow-covered trees and buildings. 'I don't even feel

40

the cold. It's as if it were powder instead of snow.'

'There's no wind to bite into you,' he said as he stacked a pile of firewood on his arm.

'What does that song call it?' she mused. 'Oh, yes, a marshmallow world. Just look at the trees! They've got sugar sprinkled on top of them, and the pine trees up the hill with those big white gumdrops weighting down their limbs!' There was no masking the delight in her face or voice. 'Logan! Look at the snowdrift by the shed!' she exclaimed with a joyous laugh.

'I was beginning to think you didn't remember my name,' he said provocatively, walking over to stand by her side as she pointed out her latest find.

She glanced up at him briefly, glad that her cheeks were already flushed by the nippy morning air and wouldn't reveal the warmth caused by the glow in his eyes.

'See how it swirls around the corner, like whipped frosting on a cake,' she said quickly.

Logan smiled affectionately as his eyes travelled over her face framed by the pale beige hood of her coat. 'You either have a very sweet tooth or you didn't eat your breakfast this morning.'

'Who wants oatmeal?' Jennifer grinned impishly. 'A big dish of fresh snow with milk and sugar sounds much better!'

'So it's snow you're wanting,' said Logan, setting the logs on the ground with a devilish gleam in his eye.

'Logan Taylor, don't you dare!' she squealed as she watched him pick up a clump of snow and pat it in his hand.

She turned just as he threw it and it splattered on her back. Quickly he started pelting her with snowballs while Jennifer fought desperately to retaliate. In seconds she was laughing and stumbling towards the cabin. A well aimed white projectile hit her in the leg, and she fell headlong into a towering snowbank. With Logan's assistance she rolled breathlessly over on to her back, giggling happily as she tried to sputter the snow out of her mouth while he laughingly brushed the snow off her face. Her hood had fallen back and the red-gold of her hair was accented by the whiteness of her headrest. The corners of his eyes were crinkled into deep lines, his dimples were deep clefts, as he rested poised above her prone body.

Suddenly the suggestiveness of her position struck Jennifer and her smile slowly sobered at the same instant his did.

'No,' she whispered as she began to struggle to get to her feet, but he quickly pinned her arms to her side.

'You've been expecting something like this ever since you met me,' he said quietly with a gleam in his eyes that Jennifer had never seen before. 'I certainly wouldn't want to disappoint you.'

Then his lips covered hers, persuasively and yet demanding a response that she wasn't willing to give. She fought the acclamation of her senses to answer the rising, hungry warmth in her body, to yield to the erratic beat of her heart. She didn't want to enjoy the possessive tenderness of his kiss. He was like Brad; she should be revolted by his embrace. But resistance only increased her desire to return the warmth and fire he was bestowing on her. In horror, she realized her lips were moving, responding to the exquisite pressure of his. Instinct had taken over while the war of logic and experience had battled in her mind.

Swiftly she turned her face away, tugging and pulling her arms free.

'He hurt you badly.' Logan studied her grimly as she moved farther away from him, scooting in the snow.

'What are you talking about?' Jennifer asked in a hoarse whisper.

'The man you left behind you.'

'No,' Jennifer answered firmly, anger flashing in her eyes. 'He didn't hurt me—my stupidity and ignorance did. I didn't recognize a wolf when he was standing in front of me. I was too blinded by charm and good looks.'

'And now?'

'And now I can see through any disguise. I just hope my sister can,' she answered sarcastically.

He stepped towards her threateningly, then halted when a jingling noise pierced the winter air. Logan turned his head away from her, exhaling slowly, before turning back to study her defiant expression.

'That'll be Carmichael. He's hitched up his horse to pull the jeep out of the snow,' he told her. 'You'd better get your things together in the cabin.' As Jennifer started to walk away, he added, 'Don't expect an apology. You enjoyed that kiss as much as I did, and if you weren't a hypocrite you'd admit it.'

She stared at him, tears stinging her eyes. Why had she let him know she was attracted by him? Why had she put such a weapon in his hands?

'Men like you always arouse the baser instincts!' Jennifer shouted in a trembling voice. 'Including self-preservation!'

Quickly she raced towards the cabin, not prepared to engage in a further battle of wits with Logan Taylor. She had salvaged a piece of her pride, and she was content with that.

After the jeep was finally freed from its snowbound bed, the short distance into Jackson, Wyoming was covered in less than twenty minutes. Patches of sunlight filtered through the thick billowy clouds to allow Jennifer to see the breathtaking mountains with black dots of trees covering their slopes. As the highway made its last curve through the mountains into the peaceful small town, she turned towards Logan, her thoughts full of questions she longed to ask even as she dreaded to break the silence.

'The town got its name from an early trapper named Jackson,' Logan informed her perceptively. 'In those early days, all valleys surrounded by mountains were called "holes" by the mountain men. Since Davey Jackson preferred trapping here over any other place, his partner referred to it as "Jackson's Hole". Gradually the "s" was dropped to make it just plain Jackson Hole.'

'What about the mountains, the Grand Tetons?' Jennifer asked, too interested in finding out more information to worry about the source. 'Did they get their names from the Indians?'

'No, as a matter of fact,' Logan replied, as he manoeuvred the jeep off the main street on to one of the side streets, 'the three highest peaks in the range were named by some French-speaking fur trappers as Les Trois Tetons, or the Three Breasts, with the largest being Le Grand Teton.'

'Oh,' Jennifer's reply was an embarrassed murmur.

'I'll take you to Sheila's house. She's probably down at the Lodge, but at least we can drop your suitcases off.' They turned a corner and slowed down in front of a picturesque pine log house. 'There's her car,' Logan went on, nodding towards a small blue car parked directly in front of them. 'Looks like you're in luck.'

A huge St. Bernard dog came bounding around the corner of the house, barking ferociously while his tail wagged frantically.

'That's the first member of your welcoming committee,' Logan smiled as he opened his door and stepped out. His smile to her had been so disturbingly male that Jennifer had remained temporarily motionless even after it had been turned away from her. She knew with sudden clarity that this would not be the last time that his stunning virility would bring a weakness to her bones. At last, his 'Down, Rags, down!' brought her hand to the door latch, and she walked around the jeep to join him.

From the same side of the house that had produced the dog now ecstatically licking Logan's face, came two more racing bundles, one in red and another in blue.

'Uncle Logan, Uncle Logan!' the blue one cried.

He was larger and faster than the red one who just reached them as the blue one flung himself into Logan's arms. 'We been so worried!'

Jennifer watched with a mixture of disbelief and wonder at the exuberant welcome, as Logan scooped the red bundle up in his other arm, gazing laughingly into the cherry red cheeks of both children.

'Mommy thaid you would come latht night,' the red one announced. The lisp immediately brought a smile to Jennifer as she recognized the face under the hood. It was Cindy.

'Your Aunt Jenny and I got stuck in a snowdrift,' Logan explained, glancing over at Jennifer with a twinkling gleam in his brown eyes. 'We had to wait until this morning before we could be pulled out. Now, where's your mother?'

'She's in the house,' said Eric as Logan set the two of them on to the ground. 'Did you stay in the snow-drift all night?'

'No, we stayed at a house nearby,' Logan answered patiently, rubbing the red hood of the other affection-ately. 'You'd better say hello to your aunt before she decides you're not even glad to see her.'

Dutifully the colourful pair turned to Jennifer and murmured their greeting. Well, she certainly couldn't expect much more, Jennifer thought. The children had only seen her a few times since Sheila had moved here. How were they to remember the hours she had held them as babies when her sister had stayed with their folks while Eric was overseas? She watched wist-fully as they raced to the house, followed by the ungainly St. Bernard. She felt Logan's gaze dwelling on her and turned.

'A little surprised by my welcome?' he mocked.

'Why should I be?' Jennifer shrugged lightly.

'They say dogs and children are instinctively right about people.'

A stinging retort rose to Jennifer's lips, but was held back as her sister came running from the house. Logan was amused at the stifling of her anger as she turned to exchange a hugging greeting with Sheila. She was grateful that Sheila took hold of the conversation, asking questions too fast to allow more than a 'yes' or 'no' answer. She had time to cool down and ignore the very nearly smirking expression on his face. Quickly they were all ushered into the house, and the suitcases were dumped unceremoniously in the centre of the tiny living room.

'There's coffee and sweet rolls in the kitchen,' Sheila announced. 'I'm sure you could do with a coffee break before lunch.'

'I'll have to take a raincheck on that, Sheila,' Logan replied. 'I'm sure Mom is worried about me, so I'd better run over there before heading out to the ranch.'

'Oh, you can call her from here,' Sheila insisted, a pleading sparkle in her striking eyes.

'As she would tell you, hearing a voice over the phone is not the same as seeing someone in person,' Logan laughed, his soft gaze trailing over Sheila's black hair down to the teasing smile on her face. 'Besides, you and Jenny will want to have some time together before you have to go to the Lodge.'

47

'Jenny?' Sheila laughed, glancing over to her sister mischievously at Logan's nickname for her. 'Oh, that must have endeared you to her heart.'

'Jenny Glenn and I,' he paused, gazing speculatively at the smouldering expression on Jennifer's face, 'have made quite an impression on each other. It was a trip I wouldn't have missed for anything.' One corner of his mouth curved mockingly. 'I'd really better go now, Sheila.'

'Don't go, Uncle Logan,' Eric begged. 'Cin and me wanted you to build a snow-fort.'

'Another time, maybe,' he answered firmly, but with a promised nod.

'Since you really must leave,' Sheila sighed, taking his hands in hers, 'then let me thank you for picking Jennifer up and bringing her here.'

Jennifer watched in gnawing agony as her sister reached up and brushed Logan's cheeks lightly with her lips. She felt her worst fears were coming true. Her sister was emotionally involved with this man. She longed to reach out and scratch his eyes when he finally turned to her in his round of good-byes.

'Good-bye, Jenny Glen. I'll see you,' he promised.

'Jenny Glenn,' Sheila echoed with a twinkle as the front door slammed behind the departing man.

'Please don't you start in with that,' Jennifer grimaced.

'I rather like it. It has a ring to it,' her sister teased. 'I wonder why we never called you that before.'

'Probably because of Mother's aversion to nicknames, which I heartily endorse.' A frown creased her smooth forehead as she turned away from Sheila. It looked as if it didn't matter what Logan did, it was all right in her sister's eyes.

'Aunt Jenny, do you want to thee my room?' Cindy asked, 'I have lotth of toyth and thingth.'

'Later, Cindy,' Sheila hushed her quickly, sensitive to her younger sister's pensiveness. 'You and Eric run out and play for a while. And for heaven's sake, take Rags with you.'

In seconds she had them bustled out the door and had turned back to Jennifer.

'Come on. Let's go into the kitchen and get some of that coffee. Then you can tell me everything,' Sheila instructed sympathetically, taking Jennifer by the arm and leading her through the living room.

Jennifer didn't tell her everything. Certainly she didn't mention her misgivings about Logan Taylor nor the embarrassing situation the previous night and the following scene in the morning. Sheila seemed to hold a very high opinion of him, one that Jennifer didn't want to alter at this time. As quickly as possible she had changed the subject of their conversation to Sheila, the children and the Lodge where Sheila worked.

Her sister had explained her hesitancy of constantly shuffling the children to Eric's parents on the weekends and as in today's case, during school vacations. His parents were quite elderly, making her two live-wires quite a handful for them. Jennifer had gladly volunteered to take care of them and fill in occasionally at the Lodge to give Sheila more free time.

In the days that followed, a pattern developed that not only brought Jennifer and her sister closer together but also Jennifer and the children. It was fun messing around in the kitchen again, fixing meals for a family, taking care of all the numerous little household chores that had grown into a burden for Sheila. As for Brad Stevenson, he quickly became a case of 'out of sight, out of mind'. Jennifer wished that Logan Taylor would be that easy. If it wasn't the children saying, 'Uncle Logan this' or 'Uncle Logan that', it was Sheila with 'Logan suggested' or 'Logan said.' No, the unwanted reminders were ever-present. But in the eight days that she had been in Jackson, Jennifer had not been subjected to his unwanted presence. She decided she should be grateful for that. At least, she wouldn't have to put up with that knowing smile of his, although she could hardly deny that his image haunted her. Naturally it was because his name was forever cropping up.

Sheila had had the afternoon free today and had insisted that Jennifer spend some time taking care of her personal chores. Since she did have some Christmas shopping still to be done, Jennifer reluctantly agreed. The children had been easy to buy for, but she wanted to take more time selecting just the right present for her sister. Her previous expeditions into town had been in the company of Cindy and Eric, who were not given to idle wondering through the stores. As it was, Jennifer had been in three stores before she found a matching sweater and slacks outfit in blue that would ideally suit Sheila.

With the gift-wrapped package under her arm, Jennifer dashed across the street to the town square where she paused briefly in front of the antlered archway that marked the path entrance through the square. She had seen it several times, but to Eric and Cindy it was old hat, not worth the extra seconds that Jennifer had longed for to study it.

The intricate network of interlocking antlers as they weaved in and out and up and over to form this strange arch amazed her. She had soon learned that antlers and trophy heads were commonplace decorations in Jackson; even the Lodge where Sheila worked had several large trophies of Big Horn sheep in the lobby, appropriately, since its name was Big Horn Lodge. But this arch was a magnificent work.

'Don't try to count them, because there's too many,' a voice behind her spoke.

Jennifer spun quickly around to see Logan Taylor standing beside her, gazing down at her with a speculative gleam in his eye.

'I wasn't counting,' she replied abruptly.

'Just admiring our quaint western novelty?' he retorted just a trifle sarcastically.

'Yes, if you must know. I find it fascinating,' Jennifer answered scathingly.

'Most people do. They're all elkhorns, you know.'

'How did they find so many?' she mused to herself, looking once again at the arch.

'It's not difficult at all, really. North of the town is the winter refuge of the elk or "wapiti", their Indian name. All the males shed their horns once a year, just

51

as the deer do,' Logan explained.

She was uncomfortably aware of his eyes on her, feeling again the quickening of her pulse.

'I heard someone mention the refuge, but I hadn't really thought too much about it. How many elk are out there?' Her voice had a nervous lilt to it as she tried to keep the conversation on an impersonal level.

'From six to eight thousand.'

'That many?' Jennifer exclaimed. 'What do they do with all the horns?'

'Only the bull elk have antlers,' Logan laughed. 'Each spring the Boy Scouts gather the antlers and have an auction here on the town square, with the proceeds going towards scouting activities.' He stopped abruptly as she turned to face him. She felt caught by his demanding gaze. 'It's cold standing here on the corner,' he finally spoke. 'Come have a cup of hot chocolate with me?'

'I . . .' she shook her head hesitantly. She didn't want to be with him, to let his maleness arouse that physical attraction she tried to stifle.

'Afraid?'

'Of course not!' Jennifer retorted, suddenly finding the voice that had forsaken her a minute ago.

'We'll go to the "public" restaurant down the street,' Logan stated with a chiding emphasis on 'public'. 'You can see the skiers come down Snow King Mountain.'

'All right,' Jennifer gave in reluctantly, unable to think of a satisfactory excuse not to go. She quickly quelled the thought that secretly she wanted to go with him. The very idea was preposterous.

His arm rested lightly and uncomfortably naturally across her waist in back. Despite the thickness of her coat she could feel the flat of his hand guiding her along.

'I see you're still wearing those silly boots,' he said, a smile teasing down at her.

'The walks are all shovelled, and it didn't seem necessary to wear my new ones,' Jennifer replied evenly.

'Then you did get some real boots.' His brown eyes glinted down on her rosy red cheeks that clashed with the coppery red colour in her hair.

'They're so bulky I feel like a lumberjack in them,' she laughed.

'And you once accused me of being vain, Jenny Glenn,' Logan baited her lightly as he turned her towards the restaurant door.

'Stop calling me that!' she answered sharply in a lowered voice, angered that she had succumbed to his easy charm and hating the skipping beat of her heart for reacting to his caressing abbreviation of her name. 'Arrogant is a better word than vain for you.'

'And here I thought that you had mellowed towards me,' he said with false regret as he pulled out a chair for her facing the window near the front. 'Absence makes the heart grow fonder and all that.'

'You've seldom been absent,' she retorted frostily as soon as Logan was seated opposite her. At the quizzical raise of his eyebrow, Jennifer explained, 'If it isn't Sheila telling me of your many virtues than it's the children raving on about "Uncle Logan". Why do they call you "uncle"? Whose idea was that?'

The waitress came at that moment, delaying Logan's answer until after he had ordered for them.

'It was the children's idea. One that neither Sheila nor I saw any harm in.' His expression was serious with a lordly tilt to his head as he answered. 'I imagine they felt they were staking a claim on me, making me an honorary member of their family. They take it seriously, and so do I.'

The waitress returned, placing before each of them a cup of hot chocolate with swirling dabs of whipped cream floating on top. Wordlessly Jennifer concentrated on hers, feeling rebuked by his statement, and knowing hers had been offered in defence of his magnetism. She glanced at him briefly, taking in the light brown sweater with the band of white circling it and the brown stag's head inside the white. There was an allusion of hardness underneath the knitted material and beneath the smiling face as well, a determination to succeed. Brad had been ambitious, too, but with a streak of cunning in him that Jennifer had just now recognized, because she suddenly realized it was absent in Logan.

'You try so hard to figure me out, Jenny. Why don't you just accept what you see?' Logan asked softly.

'Once bitten, twice shy,' she answered brightly, trying to laugh at the wariness he always aroused in her.

'Ah, but you see, I'm not trying to bite you.' Jennifer tried to catch where the slight inflection of his voice placed the emphasis, on 'bite' or on 'you'. A strange sinking feeling told her it was on the last.

'Are you saying that a worldly man like you doesn't try to score with every girl he meets?' she asked, using a smile to hide the cutting tone of her voice.

'Are you asking specifically about strawberry blondes or girls in general?' His knowing smile teased an angry fire alight in her brown eyes. 'I believe you think that kiss in the snow has branded you a fallen woman. It was only a kiss, nothing more.'

She longed to reach across the small table and slap that mocking smile off Logan's face. The anger sent a trembling through her clenched fists on the table. At his amused laugh, Jennifer flashed a burning glance towards him.

'Poor Jenny Glenn,' Logan smiled, a dancing gleam sparkling in his own eyes, 'so filled with righteous indignation! You have the innocent face of an angel, but the devil lurks behind those flames seething inside you. The truth is, I simply enjoy erasing that puritan look from your face.'

'Then let me suggest that you find someone else to have fun with, because I'm not a bit amused.' Determinedly she controlled her temper as she gathered up her bag and gloves to leave.

'Finish your chocolate, Jennifer.' Logan's expression was unchanged, but there was a hardening in his gaze indecision. He would probably be highly amused if she that momentarily halted her. An eyebrow raised at her indecision. He would probably be highly amused if she stomped out the door right now, in spite of his 'order' for her to remain, Jennifer thought. With deliberately controlled movements, she replaced her gloves and purse on the table. She averted her attention to the window where she watched the dots of skiers coming down Snow King.

'Do you ski?' Logan asked.

'Yes,' Jennifer replied calmly, her gaze remaining on the skiers as she sipped the hot chocolate.

'Do you ski well?'

'I'm an experienced amateur,' she answered.

'We'll have to make sure you get the chance to try the slopes while you're here.' Logan's voice was friendly, but Jennifer wasn't about to be drawn out by him.

'I don't require an escort to go skiing.' Her glance as it flicked over him was coolly dismissive.

She felt the amused speculation of his gaze as he replaced his cup in its saucer.

'What you really meant was you didn't require me, Jenny Glenn. But don't go up the slopes alone the first time. Have someone with you.' For all the concern in his words, the tone of his voice was completely indifferent. 'If you're ready we'll go. My car's outside, and I wanted to have a word with Sheila. Rest assured that's my only motive for taking you home.'

His suddenly casual attitude irritated Jennifer. Logan Taylor seemed to want to make it clear to her that she was of little consequence to him. Her cheeks were flushed with anger and embarrassment as they left. She could certainly treat him as lightly as he treated her.

# CHAPTER FOUR

'HERE'S the car,' Logan stated, a hand steadying Jennifer's elbow as they stepped off the pavement on to the snow-packed street.

Her gaze raised from the path of her feet to the luxurious white Continental Mark IV parked beside them. She had been expecting the jeep, and her surprise must have registered on her face.

'In the winter I store it, just taking it out a few times to keep it in condition. Besides, it's too easily lost in a white snowdrift. I have difficulty finding it,' he joked, opening the car door to assist Jennifer inside.

She couldn't help admiring the opulent black leather interior as she slid into the low seat. Her hand trailed lightly over the plush cushion as Logan walked round the car to enter on the driver's side. Quickly Jennifer placed her hand primly in her lap. She knew he was waiting for her reaction to the car. He obviously expected her to be impressed.

'I don't see how you could possibly have trouble finding it,' Jennifer smiled with saccharine sweetness. 'All you have to do is look inside to see it's as black as your heart.'

His rich, warm laugh filled the car. His gloved finger flicked her cheek lightly as he spoke. 'I knew you couldn't keep that tongue of yours still for long.'

The deeply creased lines of amusement remained in his cheeks as he started the car and backed it out of its parking place. As she stared out the side window, Jennifer mentally cursed herself. She should have known he could care less whether or not she was impressed by the car. He had waited merely to get a rise out of her, and he certainly had succeeded.

Minutes later they had arrived at their destination with Logan assisting with her packages. Instantly Logan was pounced on by the children.

'Are you bringing our Christmas presents already?' Eric demanded, his blue eyes rounded by the gaily wrapped packages in Logan's arms.

'Nope. These are presents Jenny's bought. I'm just carrying them for her,' Logan replied, ruffling the dark hair on the boy's head.

'We got our tree, Uncle Logan,' Cindy chattered brightly. 'It'th out in the wath room. Mommy thaid it had to get warm before we could decorate it. Come thee it, please.'

'You come too, Aunt Jenny,' Eric pleaded, tugging her hand.

'Jennifer,' she corrected him, with a trace of exasperation at the children's insistence on copying Logan.

'Yeth, Aunt Jenny, you come, too,' Cindy added her voice to her brother's.

'Later,' she promised. The last thing Jennifer wanted was to be confined in the close quarters of the washroom with Logan.

'Logan!' came Sheila's startled voice from the hallway. Her raven hair was piled under a towel with a few wet locks peeping out underneath. 'I didn't expect to see you this afternoon.'

'There was something I wanted to tell you.' His expression was serious as he faced Jennifer's sister, not the mockingly amused one that invariably was shown to her. 'But first, I'm off to see your tree.'

'Such as it is,' Sheila murmured to Jennifer as she watched him being hurried out of the room by her children. She glanced at Jennifer with a resigned and loving smile. 'You should see that tree! The children picked it out. On one side there's a hole two feet in diameter that's completely lacking in any branches. The rest of the tree looks as if it's suffering from malnutrition. Cindy said nobody would buy that tree, and it would be all alone on Christmas if we didn't take it. Naturally we did.'

'Naturally,' Jennifer laughed, yet touched by the totally unselfish gesture of the young child.

'All your shopping done?' her sister asked, busily putting away some of the toys scattered about as Jennifer removed her parka and hung it in the closet. 'I never dreamed you'd bring Logan home with you or I would have waited to wash my hair.'

'I ran into him downtown,' Jennifer explained hurriedly, lest her sister think she had intended to meet him. 'He insisted on giving me a ride home.'

'That was nice of him.'

'Yes,' Jennifer agreed with a noticeable lack of enthusiasm.

Her sister stared absently at the door of the washroom, her head tilted to one side in contemplation. Jennifer tucked her red-gold hair behind her ears and out of her face as she walked into the small kitchen.

'You know, sometimes I feel guilty about the way the children demand so much of Logan's attention,' Sheila mused aloud. 'But he seems to enjoy them so.' She turned abruptly towards her sister. 'Remember that game we used to play where we took the first letter of a person's name and thought of two adjectives to describe them? Every time I think about Logan, it's always "loyal," and "loving". He's done so much to help the children and me.'

The words were so far from Jennifer's 'lawless, lordly, and a Lothario' that she nearly choked.

'Want me to pour you a cup of coffee?' she hurriedly asked her dark-haired sister before the subject took a firm hold of the conversation.

'Yes, half a cup,' Logan stated, his light even tread stopping in the kitchen doorway.

'What did you think of that magnificent specimen of a Christmas tree?' Sheila laughed as she seated herself at the small wooden breakfast table in the kitchen.

'Cindy assures me it will be beautiful,' Logan said with a dubious shake of his head. 'I'm afraid some of those branches aren't heavy enough to even hold an ornament.'

He lowered his tall frame on to one of the table's chairs, spreading his legs in front of him so that Jennifer had to step across them to set the coffee down. Her hand trembled as she did so, but she refused to meet his glance. The two children entered the room as his last sentence died away.

'We can too decorate the tree and make it pretty,' Cindy insisted, hurrying over to stand beside Logan.

'But if the limbs break when we put the bulbs on,' Eric began fearfully, 'how can we decorate it?'

'We can make strings and strings of popcorn and berries and paper chains,' Jennifer spoke up quickly as the corners of Cindy's mouth began to droop.

'Just make sure that Rags doesn't decide to eat the popcorn,' Logan teased.

'Ragth hathn't theen our tree yet,' Cindy lisped with a yelp. 'Come on, Eric, leth'th go get him.'

A silence crept lightly into the room after the children had dashed outside to find their St. Bernard. Logan straightened, leaning his elbows on the table while cupping his coffee in both hands. Jennifer watched him glance speculatively at her sister before his brown head turned back to the table. He took a large drink of hot liquid before his low baritone voice spoke softly to halt the growing silence.

'I dropped into the Lodge this morning.' Logan studied Sheila out of the corner of his eye. 'You'll never guess who was checking in, Dirk Hamilton.'

Sheila's face grew as white as the towel around her head. Her hand trembled slightly as she raised her cup to her mouth in a struggle for nonchalance.

'Really?' her voice broke. 'I wonder what he's doing here at this time of the year?'

'He said he wanted to do some winterscapes of the Tetons.' Jennifer was struck by the concern that was etched in his face as Logan watched her sister's reaction. 'Listen, Sheila,' he went on quickly as she rose from the table and walked over to the sink, 'if you want me to, I'll ask him to stay somewhere else.'

'Don't be ridiculous, Logan,' put in Sheila. Too quickly, Jennifer thought, and with forced lightness. 'Why should he pay some other motel when he can pay us? Besides, it just doesn't matter to me any more. As a matter of fact I was going to take Jennifer down to the Lodge with me tomorrow, to sort of show her the ropes. It's been quite a while since the children have spent a day with Eric's parents.' Sheila paused, then she turned away from the sink and towards the intense gaze that was now fixed on her. 'Jennifer could take over some of the front desk duties.'

Jennifer suddenly felt Logan's eyes on her, his expression harsh and forbidding. She realized she was practically gaping at Sheila's statement. After all, they had only discussed her filling in on an emergency basis, if one of the maids became ill or something. Now it sounded like a full-time job. Who, in heaven's name, was Dirk Hamilton? Glancing at her sister, Jennifer saw the almost pleading expression in her blue eyes. Logan continued to stare at her, waiting for her to make some sort of comment.

'It . . . it sounds fine to me,' she stammered as Sheila silently breathed her relief. Logan didn't seem convinced of her enthusiasm, so she added, with an effort at lightness, 'I was beginning to wish for something else to do anyway. I spent an awful lot of money on schooling. It would be a shame for it to go to waste.'

'Is that the way you want to handle it, Sheila?'

Logan asked, quietly but with sharpness.

Jennifer watched anxiously as Sheila's throat worked nervously under Logan's scrutiny.

'She just said so, Logan,' Jennifer inserted quickly before her sister lost hold of her composure.

Logan's mouth closed in a grim line, accenting the tanned cheeks and firm jawline.

'I think you're making a mistake, Sheila,' was his only comment as he rose from his chair. 'I haven't the time to discuss it now.'

Jennifer was conscious of Logan's movements towards the door, even managed to indicate her thanks for the ride home, but her attention was focused on the obvious turmoil that her sister was experiencing. As the sound of the door closing behind Logan echoed into the kitchen, Sheila's movements became hurried and nervous.

'I'd better set my hair before it dries,' she said quickly, a fluttering hand touching the towel briefly.

'Who's Dirk Hamilton, Sheila?'

'Just an artist,' her sister replied—very casually. 'He was here this last summer, doing some painting.' At that moment the two children and the St. Bernard came bursting through the door. 'How many times have I told you to keep that dog out of the house when he's all muddy!' The unusually strident voice of their mother halted both children. 'You heard me. Get him out of here at once,' she ended in a more controlled voice.

The children were quick to obey. But Jennifer's heart was tugged painfully by the crestfallen and confused expressions on their young faces. A glance at Sheila told her that her sister regretted the outburst.

'Sheila?' Her hand brushed a straying strand of her red-gold bangs away from her eyes.

'Look, he was interested in some of my portraits, that's all,' Sheila said sharply, with bitterness lacing her words. 'I've never asked you to tell me about Brad, so please will you ... I just don't want to talk about it!'

For the first time that Jennifer could remember, there was a strained silence between them, one that she didn't know how to bridge and her sister refused to.

The duties outlined for Jennifer at the front desk the next morning were not difficult, but the holiday skiers made them never-ending. She couldn't suppress her curiosity about the occupant of Room 228, Dirk Hamilton, but thus far, he hadn't made himself known to the desk. She had just paused during a lull to chat with Carol, whose switchboard had also ceased to buzz insistently, when a noise from the counter drew her attention.

A man of medium height, of stocky build with thick black hair, was studying her with an analytical thoroughness from a pair of nearly black eyes. She stepped towards him, a polite smile curving her lips, when she noticed Logan enter the Lodge. His sharp brown eyes scanned the lobby quickly, coming to rest on the man in front of her. Immediately his purposeful stride brought him towards them, the lithe easiness of his swinging step surprising her with its panther-like grace.

'Good morning, Dirk.' His tanned hand reached out towards the other man in polite greeting.

'This is Dirk Hamilton,' Jennifer thought in a rather stunned silence. Although Logan was several inches taller than he, the man's hand was nearly as large as Logan's, hardly the hand and fingers of an artist. There was no masking the challenge in the gazes of either men as their eyes fixed boldly on each other. Jennifer was struck by the assured way that Logan measured the man, not overtly friendly nor hostile, but rather weighing his advantages and disadvantages should they do battle.

'I thought I'd check to see when you wanted to set up your trip into the Tetons,' Logan said casually.

'Whenever's convenient.' The answer was indifferent as was Dirk's face as he turned it back towards the silent Jennifer. His gaze travelled over her face and hair once again, cool, without apparent interest in her as a member of the opposite sex. 'You're Jennifer.'

'Y-yes,' she managed, surprised that he could possibly know who she was.

'I saw the portrait of you. Sheila couldn't capture the colour of your hair—golden like the sun with a few streaks of a fiery dusk. Copper's too brash a colour. Yours is much paler, softer, to match the smoothness of your angelic features.'

Jennifer flushed lightly at his appraisal, but flashed a warning look at the mocking gaze of Logan Taylor.

'The features may be angelic, Dirk,' Logan drawled, 'but not the girl. An angel–elf mixture would be a more appropriate description.'

'I'm Dirk Hamilton. Perhaps Sheila has mentioned me?' There was more than a hint of a question as the saturnine-faced artist offered his hand to Jennifer.

No, I'm sorry she hasn't,' she answered, placing her own slim hand in his politely. A flicker of something that resembled pain crossed his face causing Jennifer to add, 'That is, she did say you were interested in some of the portraits she's done. Is that where you saw mine?'

'Yes. Your hair was in pigtails then, much longer than it is now. There was a beguiling expression of shared laughter in your face that was very captivating,' he answered. His eyes were still busy dissecting her features, perhaps weighing them against a remembered painting.

'Oh, yes, Sheila did that one several years ago,' Jennifer smiled widely. Now that he had turned towards her, it was her turn to study his face. His features weren't handsome, but strong and powerful, yet lacking the magnetism that was so apparent in every line of Logan's face. He looked—Jennifer hesitated—dependable. Yes, that was the word, dependable.

'I take it Sheila isn't working the desk any more.' Dirk cast a cynical glance towards Logan.

'She preferred that Jenny take over this post,' Logan replied, 'at least, for the time being.'

Neither Dirk nor Jennifer missed the casual emphasis on the last phrase, leaving no doubt that the artist was the cause of the change.

Dirk's glance returned to Jennifer. This time his

inspection was more personal, including a sweep of the ringless fingers on her left hand.

'What's your opinion of artists, Jennifer,' Dirk asked.

'I'd better like them,' she answered with a flustered wave of her hand. She was irritated by the way Logan was watching her with such a disapproving glint in his eyes. She knew from the conversation between Logan and Sheila yesterday that both were upset with Dirk's sudden appearance at the Lodge. After all, she was old enough to make her own judgements about people and she rather liked this man. 'After all, my sister's an artist,' she finished before the lull became too long.

'Is she?' Dirk retorted sarcastically. 'I was under the impression that she was an innkeeper and a struggling widow with two dear children. I understood painting was a frivolous pastime to be indulged in when there was nothing left to do.'

'Dirk, why don't we go into the café and discuss your trip?' Logan suggested, intervening quickly before the stinging reply on Jennifer's lips could be heard. 'You can give me an idea of some of the places you want to go.'

Dirk removed a cigarette from his pocket and tapped it lightly on the counter before placing it between his lips.

'Yes, why don't we? Then you can begin to use your vast organizing abilities and persuasive charm to get me packed up and on my way, huh?'

Logan chuckled at the venom in Dirk's voice. It was

a rich, warm, deep sound of a man amused by the harmless barbed words flung at him. 'Your bitterness is showing,' he said as he moved aside for Dirk to precede him into the coffee shop.

A rush of pity surged into Jennifer for the over-matched artist, despite his biting criticism of her sister.

In the week that followed Jennifer was surprised at the lengths her sister went to to avoid the presence of Dirk Hamilton. She decided Sheila had a sixth sense about the man, disappearing minutes before his stocky frame entered a room. As for Dirk, the name Sheila was completely absent from his vocabulary. He always stopped and exchanged some brief conversation with Jennifer when he saw her—nothing ever personal, just passing-the-time-of-day type of talk.

What little information Jennifer had gleaned had come from Carol, the switchboard operator. She was about Jennifer's age with light brown hair and a figure that inclined towards the plump side. During different lulls in the noon and afternoon hours that Jennifer worked, it was natural that the two struck up conversation. One afternoon after Dirk Hamilton had dropped his key off at the desk with Jennifer, Carol had asked her if Sheila was glad that Mr. Hamilton had come back.

Jennifer had to reply that she really didn't know, and asked why Carol wondered if she was.

'I suppose because last summer she seemed to have such a good time with him. I mean, you'd see them having coffee or lunch together during the day, and he usually took her home at nights. For a while, some of us thought maybe there was a thing going between them,' Carol had answered rather hesitantly. 'Not that we gossiped about them or anything. It's just that your sister is such a nice person and so easy to work for. It's so sad to think about her being a widow with two children, you know, and it would be nice for her to find someone else again.'

Jennifer had agreed, then asked rather lightly the outcome.

'I guess there wasn't anything to come out of. One day he just checked out and that was it. Of course, Logan—I mean, Mr. Taylor,' the girl blushed fiercely over her error, 'was away most of the time that Mr. Hamilton stayed here.'

'What has that got to do with it?' Jennifer had questioned, seeking details of her sister's involvement with this man.

'Probably just coincidence,' Carol had shrugged lightly before leaning back in her chair to sigh. 'Mr. Taylor really is something, though. I couldn't blame your sister if she did lose her head over him. Practically everyone within a hundred miles has at one time or another, whether they'll admit it or not. He has charisma! I mean, just every girl who had anything at all going for her has drifted across his path to see if she can arouse anything in him for her.'

'And if she does?' Jennifer had had difficulty hiding the sarcasm in her words.

'Then there's a flurry of dates, with the lucky girl being the target for all those intimate smiles of his and that sensuous way he has of looking at you as if you were the only person in the room.' Carol had gazed dreamily at the switchboard while Jennifer had shivered, remembering her own reaction to his attentions. 'Lately,' Carol had continued, shaking off the illusion she had been wrapped in, 'since your sister has taken over the Lodge, the girls have got fewer and farther between. Not that anyone has conceded victory to her, you understand.'

'Of course,' Jennifer had replied, grateful that the switchboard had begun to buzz and the conversation had ended.

She tugged viciously at her hair, twisting the rubber band around half of it before glancing down at the brown, white, and black St. Bernard dog sprawled in the doorway. Lifting an eyelid, he gazed at her droopily through bloodshot eyes.

'I don't need you to tell me how juvenile I look with my hair in pigtails, Rags,' Jennifer said harshly, stepping gingerly over his legs lest he suddenly decide to rise and send her sprawling with his large hulk. 'I've got to wash out those sweaters and this hair just falls in my face.'

She hurried on past him into the kitchen where her sweaters were piled up beside the sink. Lethargically the dog rose, padded into the kitchen and flopped beside her feet.

'So you decided to keep me company.' She looked down into his mournful face, cocking her head to one side. Sighing deeply, Jennifer turned back to the sink and immersed the olive sweater in the sudsy water. 'What a way to spend my day off, in soapsuds up to my elbows and talking to a dog that's positively bored to tears! Thanks for the show of interest anyway, Rags.' The dog thumped his tail twice before closing his eyes again.

It was midweek, time to pause before the weekenders descended on the Lodge for a few days of skiing. She had planned to take care of all the time-consuming tasks that she had put off. But now that she was actually faced with doing them they all seemed so mundane.

The jingling of bells outside drifted into the house with muted tinkles. It didn't seem possible that Christmas was just next week. Not that Cindy and Eric didn't remind her often enough, and certainly not because there wasn't any snow on the ground to mar the chances of a white Christmas, because it was there in abundance. Today the holiday spirit was lacking within herself. There was no denying that there was an emptiness inside that was longing to be filled. Those jingling bells painted nostalgic pictures in her mind of childhood sleigh rides in the snow behind her father's two plough horses, Blinken and Nod. This was her first Christmas spent away from her parents, that's what had brought on the emptiness, Jennifer decided.

Refusing to let herself be drawn into a melancholy mood, she immediately began singing 'Jingle Bells' with as much robust enthusiasm she could muster. A knocking at the front door reduced the sound to a hum as she hurriedly wiped her hands dry and followed

Rags to the door.

She opened the door and her humming halted midway between 'in a one-horse open sleigh', because there, parked by the kerb, was a dark bay horse with a nervously bobbing blaze face, hitched up to a shiny black swan sleigh. Her rounded eyes turned their startled expression to the man who was braced negligently on one side of the door by an outstretched arm. She stared into a pair of brown eyes that were studying her rather lazily. Large flakes of snow drifted down between them while Jennifer continued to stare in amazement at Logan Taylor. His light brown hair had been ruffled by the breeze, and she had an inexplicable longing to reach out and smooth it into place. But the way his eyes were regarding her from beneath the gold-tipped lashes rather frightened away that thought. The wind-blown hair might have looked boyish, but the strong, tanned features were strictly male.

'Well?' Jennifer breathed unevenly, trying for a frosty indifference and settling for a melting warmth.

'Aren't your ears on straight, or is it your pigtails that are crooked?' At the teasing tilting of his head and the impish grin, Jennifer's hand rushed up to her hair.

'It's the pigtails, I imagine,' she answered, feeling the blush of embarrassment rush into her cheeks. She glanced towards the sleigh. 'Is that yours?'

'I borrowed it from a friend,' Logan replied. His eyes twinkled with amusement at her momentary discomfiture. 'I thought it would be fun to go for a ride out to the elk refuge.'

'Oh, but the children aren't home from school yet.

They won't be home for several hours. Vacation doesn't start until the weekend.'

'I know.'

'Well then, why ...' Jennifer began, only to be silenced by his laughter. She straightened indignantly. 'I don't see what's so funny?'

'I know I'm good and kind and loving,' Logan mocked, 'and a perfect example for the children. But this afternoon I decided to play the role you prefer to see me in—the wolf to Little Red Riding Hood.' He tugged a red-gold pigtail mischievously. 'Or would you prefer to be my Rudolph and guide my sleigh for me?'

She hesitated, her gaze on the horse and sleigh and her mind picturing a ride through the snow. But with Logan? Wasn't that asking for trouble?

'Well, Jenny Glenn? Dolly's getting impatient. Will you come with me?' His low voice added its own persuasive magic.

'Yes,' she answered quickly and breathlessly before she could change her mind.

'Hurry up, then. Get your coat. I'll wait for you by the sled.' The brown stetson that was firmly placed on the gold-brown hair before Logan retreated from the door.

With a quickness that surprised her, Jennifer grabbed her blue maxi coat out of the closet, stuffed a pair of mittens in the pocket, pulled on her snow-boots, and snared a pair of ear-muffs as she bustled Rags out the door ahead of her. Logan was waiting beside the sleigh to give her a hand on to the seat. She was pulling her mittens on as he crawled up beside her from the opposite side. He reached down and unfolded a heavy horsehair blanket. The seat wasn't very wide, and Jennifer stiffened as his arm brushed her. With a barely concealed smile, he handed her a corner of the blanket, his gaze encompassing the apprehensive expression on her face.

'Here, tuck this in around your side,' he instructed. 'It'll keep the draught off your legs.'

She did as she was told while he took the opposite end and tucked it around himself before taking the reins and clicking to the horse. The first few blocks, Jennifer was uneasily aware of the man beside her, the touch of his arms and legs against hers, but gradually she relaxed to the cheerful ringing of the bells on the horse's harness. The large petal flakes of snow seemed to float in the air around them mixing aimlessly with the puffy clouds from their own breath. Then they were out of town, the sleigh's runners skimming effortlessly over the snow-packed road.

# CHAPTER FIVE

THE magic silence of the falling snow filled Jennifer with a mystical sense of going back in time. The foothills of the mountains closed in around them, their tops hidden by the low cloud cover. She didn't even have to close her eyes to capture the feeling of long ago days.

'Can't you just picture what it was like years ago?' Jennifer whispered very low, almost fearing to break the spell. 'Before cars and civilization moved in?'

'Mother Earth,' Logan agreed quietly. 'With all the untouched beauty of a virginal girl. Would you have enjoyed being a pioneer?'

'Only if I were a boy!' She grimaced playfully at him.

'So you prefer being a liberated woman.' His eyes danced teasingly over her face.

'You don't object, surely?' With a merry glint in her own eyes. 'Or are you a male chauvinist?'

'Those are fighting words in Wyoming, girl.' Logan eyed her in mock dismay. 'Has your education been so neglected that you didn't know Wyoming is the "Equality State"? This was the first state in the Union to grant political, civil, and economic equality to women back when we were still a territory. You'll find that Wyoming men know the value of a good woman, not just as a housewife and mother of our children, but as a person to stand by our side.'

Jennifer remained silent when he finished, stunned by his unexpected endorsement of the female species.

'What's the matter, Jenny Glenn? Aren't those words you expected to hear from a womanizer?' She couldn't help flushing at his astuteness. 'Despite all our arrogant boasting to the contrary, we men require a woman to fulfil the demands of our soul as well as to satisfy the needs of our flesh.' A shiver raced up Jennifer's back at his words. Could he feel that way about a woman? she thought, glancing at him from the corner of her eye. His profile beneath the wide brim of his stetson hat was deeply etched against the white backdrop. His expression was pensive as he felt her gaze and turned to meet it. His brown eyes seemed much darker as they reached out to hold hers captive. Her pulse increased at an alarming rate as the corners of his mouth curved into the most tender smile. Quickly she averted her face before she revealed too much of what she was feeling.

'That sounds like an apt description of love, Logan.' She spoke brightly in an effort to halt the tumultuous hammering of her heart. 'Are you on speaking terms with this emotion?'

His answering chuckle was short but rich with amusement.

'Would it appeal to your quixotic heart if I said I was waiting for the ghost of a former lover to fade before revealing my feelings to the one I cherish and adore? No, I can see by the stricken look on your face that you wouldn't believe a tale like that. Not that you wouldn't like to see me brought to my knees by a woman.' Logan pulled the horse to a halt, then turned sideways in the seat, laying an arm along the back near Jennifer. Two smug dimples winked over at her. 'My mother says I'm sampling the fruits so that at harvest time I'll be able to pick the most delectable one.'

'That's the most pompous reasoning I've ever heard.' Her mind was not willing to ignore his first response about the ghost of a former lover. Could he possibly have been referring to Sheila's late husband, Eric?

'Oh, it's not so bad. Isn't that what these parrying and thrusting conversations between the sexes are all about? To see if there's more than just physical chemistry? Look at the two of us. There's a certain combustible mixture between us. A rousing of the baser instincts, I believe you once called it,' Logan stated, alluding back to their battle of words after the kiss in the snow. Anger swept through Jennifer, stiffening her back and tilting her head defiantly. 'Perhaps I should ask if you've been in love before. Or was that man back in Minneapolis just an experiment at love to see how deep your emotion for him was?'

'That's none of your business!'

'It couldn't have been love because I only see anger in your eyes,' deriving amusement once again out of her display of temper. 'There seems to be no lasting wound.'

'How could Sheila have the nerve to tell you about that?' Jennifer fumed.

'Believe me, I only received the sketchiest of details, and that was because I was there when you phoned.'

She eyed him sceptically and in spite of his exaggerated air of innocence, she believed him. Mostly because she didn't think her sister could be that unfeeling of Jennifer's privacy to tell a complete stranger the entire story.

'What were you doing with Sheila at that hour ... sampling fruit?' Sarcasm coated every word.

'Darling Jenny,' Logan sighed, 'that kind of a statement is more slanderous to your sister's reputation than to mine.'

'I thought you said there wasn't any double standard in Wyoming for women,' Jennifer observed with deadly amusement. Inwardly she regretted the smear to her sister, but outwardly she couldn't resist another jibe at his male ego.

'We recognize equality, but we honour propriety.' Logan's amused exasperation was beginning to show the edges of anger, even though carefully controlled. 'A hangover from the pioneer days, too, I suppose, when chivalry was an admirable trait and the fairer sex was respected.'

The horse moved restlessly against the traces, no longer content to stand patiently in the snow. Logan slapped the reins lightly on her rump, and the horse started off at a slow trot. The horse-drawn vehicle passed several sheds filled with hay before Jennifer was able to swallow enough pride to speak.

'I apologize. I spoke out of line back there, and I just want you to know I'm grateful for everything you've done for Sheila – and the children.'

'And I apologize for taunting you so.' The full charm of his smile was turned on her as his hand, resting on the back of the seat, reached out and tugged her hair. 'But then you were being a little impertinent.' His hand rested momentarily on her shoulder, sending breathless shivers of heat through her before it returned to aid the other one in slowing the horse to a walk. Logan's gaze was now directed in front of them. 'We've reached our destination, Jenny. There's your elk.'

She had been so completely engrossed in their conversation and aware only of the man beside her that she had paid no attention at all to their surroundings. Looking forward, Jennifer saw a large blotch of brown in the distance. Nearer to them was another hayshed and a smaller building with two wagons and teams of horses standing beside it.

'The Jaycees and the refuge, in a co-operative effort, operate a sleigh ride to the elk herd,' Logan explained following her questioning gaze.

A man walked out of the small building and waved a friendly hello to them. Logan reined their horse to a halt and waited until the man walked up to their sleigh.

'Hello, Frank,' Logan smiled. 'I thought I'd take Miss Glenn for a closer look at the herd.'

'Fine, fine,' the man smiled. 'Probably won't be able to get too close, though. They're still kinda skittish, and especially so of a strange sled.'

'Thanks, we'll be careful,' Logan nodded before clicking to the horse.

As they drew closer, Jennifer was able to distinguish individual animals amidst the sea of brown. Some were lying down; some were standing; some were grazing; and some were watching their approach. She sat in awed silence studying the grey-brown bodies with their chestnut manes and straw-coloured rumps. Two females reared at each other, hooves striking out, disputing ownership of a salt block. A big bull elk with an enormous rack of antlers eyed them haughtily.

'In Europe these animals are known as moose, although you can see they bear no resemblance to the animal we call moose. The males stand about five feet tall at the shoulder and top out at about a thousand pounds. The females are smaller. The males you see with the short, spiked antlers are usually one or two years old. The older bulls will have five or six points on each antler.' Logan's low voice came from just behind her ear.

'Where do they all come from?' Jennifer wished the unsettling awareness of how close he was to her would go away.

'Mostly from the Yellowstone and Grand Teton National Parks to the north. At the first good snow they migrate down here to the refuge.'

'Have they always come here?'

'No, they used to travel further south to the plains around Rock Springs. In the 1880s when ranching operations cut their winter forage to practically nothing, both here in Jackson Hole and elsewhere, they began starving to death. One spring it was said you could walk for miles on the carcasses of dead elk. Plus the elk had to contend with hunters called tuskers, who killed them only for their teeth, which were highly prized by the Elk Lodge. That was finally outlawed and the refuge established by Congress in 1913.'

An eerie, yapping wail broke out from the hillside, joined by several other equally mournful voices. The uncanny howl, like an animal in pain, sent shivers down Jennifer's spine. She glanced at Logan apprehensively.

'Don't you like the serenade? It's coyotes. They're the sanitarians of the wild, cleaning up the carcasses of dead animals.'

'Don't they attack the herd?'

'They don't need to. There are always crippled and wounded elk that make their way to the refuge after hunting season. Some make it through the winter, but others are too weak to survive. Others die simply from old age. The coyotes and other scavengers like the raven live very well.'

'How horrible!' Jennifer shuddered expressively.

'Just the balance of Nature,' Logan reasoned, but with a sympathetic smile. 'Look there on the hillside.' His arm reached around her to point. She trembled, but this time not because of the coyotes. 'You can see our dubious choir there by that stand of pines.'

She looked obediently in the direction, knowing that he must be able to feel the quaking of her body even through her coat.

'Are you cold, Jenny?'

Her heart leaped at his words and the sudden tightening of his arm around her shoulder. Although she stiffened slightly, he pulled her closer to him, his hand rubbing her shoulders briskly.

'We'd better head for home and get you in front of a warm fire,' he said calmly, either ignoring her resistance or unaware of it as he urged the mare into a trot. 'Very rarely do you see other animals in the refuge,' Logan continued conversationally. 'Deer and moose usually find their own forage in the Park or migrate south. Sometimes you see the rare trumpeter swan on the refuge waters. They spend the year here. There's a fish hatchery as well, but we'll see that another time.'

Jennifer nodded a silent agreement, resolving inwardly that she wasn't going to subject herself to this type of an intimate excursion again. He was too physically attractive for her peace of mind.

They made the circle in silence past the small building housing the concession ride with Logan, raising a hand in good-bye to the man named Frank. Once again the jingling bells on the horse's harness were the only sounds heard in the silence of a wintry afternoon. The shiny black sleigh with its curving sides seemed to snuggle its two riders in its lap. Jennifer romantically pictured herself resting against Logan's side, his arm hugging her to him. She blamed the idea on the old-fashioned setting and not on any desire on her part for such a scene to take place with Logan.

His gloved hand moved to rest on the side of her neck, caressing it affectionately.

'You can rest your head on my shoulder if you want,' Logan suggested.

Jennifer's eyes flashed resentful sparks of anger at

him. Trust him to know that she had just thought of the singularly inviting idea herself!

'I'm perfectly all right, thank you,' she said firmly, moving as far away from him as the small seat would allow, which wasn't very far.

'What's the matter? Are you afraid I had designs on your virtue?' His seductive glance played havoc with her pulse.

'No, I was merely assuring you that I was warm enough and comfortable enough not to need to make use of your—your——'

His bewitching smile melted her attempt at cool composure and he finished her sentence for her. 'Shoulder is the word.'

'I know,' Jennifer retorted indignantly. She was only too aware that he knew exactly what effect he had upon her senses. She maintained silence the rest of the ride back to the house.

'Well, Jenny Glenn, here we are, safe and sound.' Logan baited her roguishly as he reined the horse to a stop in front of Sheila's.

He stepped down off the sleigh and turned to place his hands firmly around her waist before lifting her to the ground. She stared angrily up at his bemused expression as he failed to release her from the circle of his arms. Breathlessly she saw his gaze fasten on her lips. For one horrifying moment she thought he was going to kiss her. His sensuous masculine lips hovered invitingly above hers, reminding her how vulnerable and responsive she had been the last time that they had exquisitely possessed hers with a wild sweetness.

'I had a very nice time, Logan,' she rushed in hurriedly, knowing her inner confusion made her words sound stiff and insincere.

'As much as you would allow yourself,' Logan laughed. His gaze shifted from her lips to encompass her entire face with an amused detachment. His hands returned to his side and she was free.

'It never hurts to be on one's guard,' Jennifer retorted scathingly, stepping away from him before he changed his mind about having released her.

'Tell Sheila that I'll be out of town for the next day or two, will you?' he asked without rancour. 'When I get back, I'll probably have to spend a few days at the ranch. Unless I hear from her otherwise, Mother and I will be over about seven on Christmas Eve.'

'Christmas Eve?' Jennifer questioned in stunned surprise. 'What are you coming over for?'

'Mother and I usually come over for an hour or so on Christmas Eve,' he frowned. 'It's been a tradition in our family since Eric and I were boys in school.'

'I didn't know.' Jennifer's reply was an apologetic whisper. The nearly burning resentment in his eyes had startled her. She was so accustomed to the charming side of him that she had forgotten until this moment how dominatingly displeased he could become, and she didn't like being the object of his displeasure. 'We'll look forward to seeing you Christmas Eve, then,' Jennifer said calmly and with dignity.

'Till then,' Logan agreed with a half smile of politeness.

Jennifer passed Logan's message on to Sheila that

evening. Her sister admitted in an offhand manner that it was something that they had done every year, confirming Logan's assertion.

'If you like, the children and I always get them a gift every year, nothing too expensive, but we can add your name to the card,' Sheila had suggested.

'No. ...' Jennifer had hesitated, a rebellious, devilish idea forming in her head. 'I think I'd rather pick out a gift for Logan myself.'

'As for Mandy, Logan's mother, you can always play it safe by getting her the latest best-seller.'

'Mmmm, thanks,' Jennifer had replied absently, hugging her secret plans to herself in malicious glee.

It was three days later before she was finally able to have a free afternoon. Jennifer had no difficulty locating Mrs. Taylor's present. Taking Sheila's advice, she had gone to the local bookstore and discovered them in the midst of unpacking the latest best-sellers and chose a biography. She also found a very delicately filigreed metal bookmarker which she also purchased. With the simple task done, she went in search of Logan's present. Several stops later she finally found what she was looking for. She was nearly bubbling with laughter as she watched the sceptical clerk wrapping it up for her.

Leaving the store, Jennifer glanced at her watch. Sheila was to pick her up in less than an hour. Time enough to have a leisurely cup of coffee at the restaurant.

She chose the little café that Logan had taken her to, for no other reason, she told herself, except that it was close at hand. It was quite crowded with skiers who were beginning to call it a day on the slopes. The only free table she could see was a small one for two off in the corner. She was half finished with her coffee when she happened to look up and notice Dirk Hamilton walk in the door. By chance he spotted her at almost the same instant. He glanced around the full tables, then back at Jennifer, and hesitated before striding over to the table.

'Would you object to sharing the table with me, Jenny?' Dirk asked politely, almost steeling himself for her refusal.

'Of course not,' she smiled.

He managed a half smile of gratitude before he settled his stocky frame in the chair opposite her. For some reason his calling her Jenny didn't ruffle the hair in the back of her neck. The way Logan said it always made it sound like a substitute for 'darling'.

'You don't mind me calling you Jenny, do you?' Dirk questioned after ordering a cup of coffee. 'The name Jennifer always conjures up the image of a sophisticated person for me, and there's not a trace of artificialness about you.'

'I'll take that as a compliment, thank you,' Jennifer laughed. 'Strangely enough it's only since I've come to Jackson that people have shortened my name. I resented it a great deal at first.'

'I've noticed that Logan Taylor calls you Jenny.' A bitter smile played across his lips. 'Was it the name you resented or the person using it?'

'Since he's played such an active role in my sister's life, I think I'll let that question pass.'

'I detect a lack of endorsement of the indomitable Mr. Taylor in your statement.' Dirk eyed her curiously. 'Doesn't his charm work its magic on you?'

'I'm just not taken in by it,' Jennifer asserted. Her basic honesty refused to let her lie about the physical attraction he aroused in her. 'Sheila is another question.'

'Sheila is blinded by his security,' Dirk sighed. Exasperation and anger mingled with his words. 'His material security.'

'Raising two children on your own usually forces a person to look at the financial side of life.' Jennifer spoke up firmly, not liking the picture Dirk was painting of her sister as a gold-digger.

'And an artist can rarely offer much promise of that, can he?' It was a rhetorical question that lapsed into silence as Dirk stared moodily at the table. Finally when the waitress had returned with his coffee, Dirk looked up at Jennifer, a very determined expression on his square-jawed face. 'When I first started out painting, I had to prostitute a lot of my work to survive. I'm thirty-five years old, Jenny. Between exhibits and commissions, I've passed that early stage of struggle. I make a fairly adequate living.'

His big fist slammed the table to emphasize his words. He glanced around him in embarrassment, then ran his hand through the dark thatch of his hair.

'But your sister has reduced me to the stage of a

puppy dog, running in circles chasing his tail,' Dirk added grimly. 'There's no painting I particularly want to do here. It's all just an excuse. I take it she never talks about me to you?'

Jennifer shook her red-gold head negatively.

'I fell in love with her last summer, and I thought Sheila fell in love with me, too. I mean the kind of love where you accept the person the way they are. But all of a sudden she was talking about me getting a job and painting on the side. The financial future of an artist was too uncertain for her. She wanted to know there was money coming in every week, without being dependent upon the whims of the buying public. It didn't matter to her that painting was my life and my future. All those idyllic days were swept away by vicious arguments. I left, telling myself I was lucky to be rid of her and her materialistic world. I told myself she was better off with Logan, and in time, I'd get her out of my system.'

'But you couldn't convince yourself,' Jennifer stated softly.

'No,' Dirk agreed in a quiet, resigned voice. 'I had to come back one last time. So far, I haven't even seen the back of her head. My God!' he exclaimed suddenly, 'why am I unburdening all this on you!'

'I have a very sympathetic ear.' Jennifer's heart went out to her tortured companion. 'Besides, who would make a better conspirator than the victim's sister?'

'I couldn't let you do that.' The light that had flickered so hopefully in his dark eyes blinked out. 'I wouldn't want to put you in the position of being disloyal to your family.'

'How would I be doing that?' she quipped. 'The idea of Logan as Sheila's husband sends chills down my back. I would just be looking out after my sister's interests by introducing someone I thought more suitable back into her life.'

'You've set yourself out a demanding task. She's been making it perfectly clear that she doesn't want to see me.' Dirk shook his head ruefully, gradually being drawn into Jennifer's plot despite his misgivings.

'She certainly can't stop me from having my friends over, unless she kicks me out of the house, which I doubt. And if she should happen to be at home when you come over, well...?' Jennifer ended with a mischievous twinkle in her eye.

'You're a conniving little witch.' But the smile on his face was so wide and such a marked change from the sullen, sober expression that Jennifer broke into a lilting laugh.

'I found her, Mommy!' a childish voice cried just before two red-parkaed arms flung themselves around Jennifer.

'Cindy, I didn't expect to see you,' Jennifer exclaimed in surprise.

'We been lookin' all over for you,' Cindy admonished as Jennifer glanced up to see Sheila and Eric making their way over to the table. Evidently Sheila hadn't seen her companion as yet.

'Hello, Cindy,' Dirk said quietly.

She turned a pair of startled blue eyes on him before breaking into an enormous smile and dashing over to his side.

'Oh, Dirk, I mithed you tho,' she lisped, her little voice trembling with emotion. 'Mommy thaid you'd never come back.'

'I thought I taught you how to say your S's,' Dirk stated, a mock reprimand sparkling out of his dark eyes.

'Sssss,' Cindy went. A sad almost lonely expression came on to her face as she enunciated very clearly, 'It didn't seem very important after you left us.'

Dirk never replied to her statement because he had just glanced up into Sheila's white face. Jennifer was amazed at the lack of expression in his face and voice as he greeted her quietly.

'Hello, Sheila. How are you?'

Sheila glanced numbly at her sister before mumbling that she was fine. Dirk turned to a very sulky-looking Eric.

'And how's my little man?'

'I'm not your little man!' Eric retorted sharply, stepping away from the hand reaching out to him.

'Aren't you glad Dirk is back, Mommy?' Cindy cried, then turned excitedly back to him. 'You should thee Ragth. He'th real big and fat now! You know what we bought him for Chrithmath? A toy pork chop! Ithn't that nithe!'

'Hush, Cindy!' Sheila's face was incredibly flushed as she met Dirk's glance. 'I'm sure Mr. Hamilton isn't interested in that.'

'Yes, he ith tho, aren't you, Dirk?' Cindy insisted.

'Of course,' he answered calmly, raising an eyebrow in Sheila's direction.

Cindy flicked her mother an 'I-told-you-so' glance before continuing. 'You should thee what I bought Eric. We're gonna open our prethenth Chrithmath Eve. Oh, I wish you could be there. Our tree ith tho beautiful.'

'Isn't that strange you should say that, Cindy?' Jennifer inserted quickly. 'I was just asking Dirk what his plans were for Christmas Eve, and he said he hadn't a thing to do. He was going to be all alone.'

She knew it was unfair using the child to further her plans, but Jennifer knew she would do anything to wrest her sister away from the clutches of Logan Taylor.

'Jennifer!' Sheila exclaimed in a horrified whisper with an angry, accusing gleam in her eyes.

'Do come, Dirk. Pleathe!' Cindy pleaded.

'Of course I'll come,' Dirk said, then loooked over at Jennifer. 'If you're sure it's all right?'

'Seven o'clock in your best holiday attire!'

'It's a date,' Dirk smiled.

'Good. Well, I imagine you're ready to go,' Jennifer said to Sheila. 'I'll probably see you tomorrow, Dirk.'

The silence of Eric and Sheila was hidden by the chorus of good-byes exchanged among Cindy, Jennifer, and Dirk. They were out on the street when Sheila managed a very angry 'How could you?' to Jennifer which she shrugged off indifferently. After all, she had invited Dirk for her sister's own good. It was certainly nothing to do with needing a shield for herself from Logan's presence. Or was it?

# CHAPTER SIX

It was the night before Christmas Eve and Jennifer had tucked Cindy and Eric into their beds more than a half hour ago. Sheila was still at the Lodge, working. Sheila. If anyone would have told Jennifer a week ago that there would be such a strained silence between them, she would have laughed. She had expected her sister to explode after the invitation to Dirk, thus allow Jennifer to use all her well-thought-out arguments. But her raven-haired sister had discovered a better weapon. Her silence was a much more eloquent accusation of betrayal, one that didn't allow Jennifer the opportunity for discussion.

With a sigh of annoyance, Jennifer closed the book that had failed to capture her attention. She gazed at the twinkling lights on the Christmas tree. They really had done a good job of decorating the spindly thing. It had taken hours of stringing popcorn by the two children and two sisters before they had enough garlands to fully circle the tree. Many of the ornaments had been too heavy, as Logan had decreed, but there had been some that they were able to use, which, with the aid of a few hand-made snowflakes, had dressed it out nicely in its holiday garb. A few applications of artificial snow had hidden the worst of the bare spots. And now with the twinkling fairy lights, it looked quite festive.

Restless stirrings from Eric's room quickly switched her thoughts back to Sheila and Dirk. It hadn't taken Jennifer long to discover that Eric's sullenness marked him as a second adversary in her desire to bring her sister and the artist together. But his reticence in accepting Dirk was all the more confusing when compared with Cindy's wholehearted endorsement.

She rose from the armchair and tiptoed quietly to his door to check on him. As her shadow filled the doorway, Eric turned his head towards her, a pair of wide-awake, questioning blue eyes studying her.

'Can't get to sleep?' she asked softly, not wishing their voices to wake Cindy in the next room. 'Is something troubling you, Eric?' He still failed to reply. 'Sometimes if you talk about it, your problem doesn't seem as bad when it's shared.'

He rolled over so that he was facing her as Jennifer walked over to sit beside him on the bed. She could tell he was mulling over her words, trying to decide if he wanted to tell her.

'I'll be glad to listen.'

He looked at her solemnly.

'Does God really hear everybody's prayer? Even a little kid's?'

'Most especially little children's,' Jennifer asserted with a smile.

'Does He always answer them?'

'Oh, yes. He always answers them, but sometimes, Eric, the answer is "no".' His shoulders drooped at her words, and his chin settled down on his chest. 'What was your prayer for?'

Two very sad blue eyes looked up at her with a hint of rebellion lurking in the darkness of his pupils.

'I prayed that Logan would marry Mommy.' There was no masking the defiance of his voice. 'And that Dirk would go away and never come back.'

Jennifer managed to smother her exclamation of dismay and reply calmly. 'That wouldn't be very fair to your sister. She likes Dirk, you know.'

'She's just a baby.' Eric's chin trembled at his effort to hold back the two giant tears that were forming in his eyes. 'The only reason she likes him is because he gave us Rags. He was just a dog that nobody wanted.'

'That's not true any more. Rags has a very good home here. I know Cindy loves him dearly, and I think you do too.'

'I do not! He's ugly and clumsy and a coward! I want a dog like the one Logan has at his ranch. He's got a job and he's important. Uncle Logan says he could never take care of all those cattle without Ranger!'

'Logan again,' Jennifer grimaced silently.

'St. Bernards are very brave dogs, Eric. They've been used for years in Europe to rescue people lost in the snow. You should be proud of Rags, because his ancestors saved many people from blizzards and avalanches.'

'I guess I like Rags all right.' He admitted reluctantly. But the brief flicker of interest her words had sparked was replaced quickly by sullenness. 'But I still don't like Dirk!'

'But why?' Jennifer cried in a puzzled exclamation.

'Because the last time he was here, he made Mommy cry! And I don't want her to cry again.' His last words ended in a painful sob.

'Oh, Eric,' she murmured, reaching out her arms to the tortured little boy as he hurled himself into them. Holding the sobbing small body against her breast, Jennifer wondered how she could possibly explain to her nephew that Logan was more capable of making Sheila cry, too. As his weeping subsided gradually, she smoothed the dark hair on his tousled head and began to explain, 'People cry for all sorts of reasons. Because they're hurt or lonely or even because they're happy. You mustn't be too hard on Dirk. He may have made your mommy cry, but he also could make her very happy. That's what you want, isn't it? For her to be happy?' His dark head nodded slowly while his little hand manfully brushed away his tears. 'So why don't we just wait and see what happens, okay?'

'Okay, Aunt Jenny,' he agreed quietly, moving out of her arms and back on to his bed.

'Do you think you can go to sleep now?'

'Yes.' He snuggled under the covers. 'I do feel better, too.'

'I'm glad,' Jennifer smiled, silently wishing that she did. 'Good night, then. Sleep tight and don't let the bed-bug's bite,' she teased, dropping a light kiss on his forehead.

'Good night.'

At the rap on the door, Jennifer removed the organdie frilled apron that she was wearing to protect her long green velvet gown. The slender flowing lines of the dress softly accented her youthful curves while the deeply cut V-neck showed off her swan-like neck. The long sleeves, fitting the upper portion of her arms before fanning out gracefully around her wrists, gave the gown a slightly medieval effect. She had coiled her hair into a coronet of curls on top of her head which added to the image.

She opened the front door to admit Dirk, whose arms were laden with gaily wrapped Christmas packages.

'Merry Christmas!' he smiled widely.

'You must be Santa Claus,' she teased as he managed to juggle a few of the packages into her arms. 'Eric! Would you come here? You have some more presents to put around the tree.'

With the gifts safely distributed between Eric and Cindy, Jennifer helped Dirk off with his coat.

'I kept expecting you to call me this afternoon and tell me not to come,' Dirk began nervously as he looked into the front room where the two children had engaged their grandparents' help in placing the packages around the tree. 'Where's Sheila?'

'In the kitchen, as silent as a mummy.' She raised her eyebrow in an expressive shrug just as there was a knock at the door.

'That'll be Logan,' said Dirk. 'They were just driving up when I knocked at the door.'

Jennifer reluctantly opened the door and exchanged

holiday greetings with Logan and the exceedingly charming woman who was his mother, before calling out to her sister.

'Sheila, Logan and Mrs. Taylor are here!'

There was a quick flurry of feet as Cindy and Eric descended on the pair, quickly relieving them of the burden of their packages. During that time, Jennifer had a few seconds to study Mrs. Taylor. She had half expected to meet an autocratic woman who doted on her son to the exclusion of everyone else. Her opinion was quickly revised when she looked into the crinkly brown eyes above the dimpled smile.

But her inspection was halted by the sharp intake of breath from Dirk as her sister entered the room. The clinging knit pants suit with its widely belled legs was only a shade lighter than her brilliant blue eyes. Even her hair falling in a dark cloud around her shoulders glistened with a blue-black sheen. Jennifer couldn't prevent herself from glancing at Logan to see if his reaction to her sister was as marked as Dirk's, only to find him inspecting her. She took an involuntary step closer to Dirk in protection, hearing Logan's words of introduction of her to his mother in a muted fog.

'Jenny Glenn. What an unusual and lyrical name!' His mother's voice called her back to reality. 'But it suits you perfectly. I look on your sister as an adopted daughter which makes you part of our family, too, so I insist that you call me Mandy.'

It was impossible for Jennifer not to feel immediately warmed by this woman. In her own way, she was just as charming as her son, only instinctively Jennifer knew she was sincere while she still had many doubts about Logan's motives.

Taking the fur-trimmed coat of Mrs. Taylor, Jennifer added it to Dirk's already draped over her arm and led the exodus into the living room. She was nearly to the hall doorway that led to the bedroom where they were keeping the wraps of the guests when she noticed Eric tugging Logan's arm insistently. Intuitively she knew his reason for whispering in Logan's ear had nothing to do with childish talkativeness. She and Logan simultaneously followed the path pointed out by the small finger, both pair of eyes coming to rest on the sprig of mistletoe dancing festively from a string above Sheila's head. Jennifer's lips compressed tightly. Her nephew was proving to be a very worthy opponent.

'You have a romantically inclined son who believes in Christmas traditions being carried out,' Logan declared after he had walked over to Sheila, tapped her on the shoulder and pointed above her head. 'And I don't pass up any invitation to kiss a beautiful woman.'

In the brief moment that Logan held Sheila's lips captive in a tender kiss, Jennifer was jolted by a never-before-known surge of jealousy. Amidst the teasing cheers that marked the end of the kiss, Logan's eyes met hers. All too aware that her emotions must be written on her face, she spun quickly away and hurried into the hallway and on to the bedroom. She dropped the coats quickly on the bed and clutched at the footboard to support her suddenly shaking legs.

It was preposterous! her mind sang out. That she

could be jealous of Logan kissing her sister! It was out of the question! She despised the man, hated and despised him! It had to have been anger. Yes, anger—brought on by a combination of Eric's childish manipulations and Logan's natural Don Juan tendencies. Oh, God, please let it be anger! she cried silently to herself.

'Is this where the coats go?'

Still clutching tightly to the bed-rail, Jennifer pivoted swiftly around to face Logan. His glance flicked passed her to the bed.

'I guess it must be,' answering his own question with a half smile. She watched him warily as he walked closer, stopping in front of her while tossing his coat past her on to the bed. She tried desperately to meet his gaze coolly. 'I had the distinct impression a few minutes ago that you wanted to scratch somebody's eyes out. Mine or Sheila's?'

'I think your ego is showing,' Jennifer retorted, fighting the breathlessness in her voice.

'Could be.' His head moved to one side indifferently, but his gaze remained on her pale face and trembling lips. 'I had decided you were too shy to share the chaste pleasures of a kiss under the mistletoe in a room full of people, and were seeking a more private place.' At her angry indrawn breath, he added, his tongue very definitely in cheek, 'But I dismissed that idea as being too inviting a suggestion from such an inviolate maiden. Did you know that shade of green makes your hair seem more red than gold?' he commented with a lightning change of subject.

'I'm sorry you don't like it,' Jennifer retorted sarcastically. He was going too fast for her and she was too weak to keep up with him. No longer capable of meeting his gaze, she turned her back on him.

'I like it.' His low voice had a smooth seductive quality to it now. His hand suddenly began caressing the back of her neck lightly. 'I've heard that near the base of the neck is the most vulnerable place to heighten a woman's desire. Is that true?'

His fingertips were leaving a trail of fire that was rapidly beginning to course through her body.

'Stop it!' she hissed, spinning quickly around to face him before she lost control. His hand rested now alongside her throat.

'Your pulse is racing,' he drawled with the most irritating calmness considering the massive turmoil Jennifer was in.

She stared into his mocking brown eyes. He knew exactly what he was doing to her and the knowledge that he knew infuriated her.

'I despise you!' she sobbed as she shoved his hand away. 'You're ... you're everything that's loathsome in a man. Every woman you meet must become a trophy for your ego!'

'It's amusing how righteously sure of yourself you are, and still you're attracted to me.' His whole demeanour was quietly composed as he gazed down at her in fascination.

'Attracted!' Jennifer cried. 'Repelled is a better word.'

'I can see we're going to have a very stormy relationship,' Logan laughed.

She spluttered angrily for a moment before flouncing out of the room. By the time she reached the living room, her temper was under control and only her hands clenched into tight fists betrayed her inner fury. She quietly shifted Cindy from her seat on the sectional couch beside Dirk to her lap, avoiding Logan's amused glanced when he followed her into the room after a discreet pause. The soothing sounds of 'Adeste Fidelis' and other Christmas carols that Sheila had placed on the record player eventually calmed her to the point where she could join in with the rest of the festive group. Sheila and Dirk, although seated across the room from one another, were on speaking terms.

'Peace' had always been Christmas's theme, she thought, casting a thankful glance at the lack of hostilities between her sister and Dirk. She glanced resentfully towards Logan, who was listening very attentively to Mr. Jeffries, Sheila's father-in-law, but she certainly didn't feel any 'goodwill towards men' tonight.

'Ithn't it time to open our prethents?' Cindy asked for the sixth time.

'I agree with Cindy.' Mrs. Taylor spoke up from the chair on Jennifer's right. 'It's time to end the suspense.'

'All right, all right,' Sheila laughed after being beseiged by two concurring children. 'Grandpa Paul, will you do the honours and distribute the presents?'

As the gifts were passed around, the small living room became a chaotic confusion of brightly coloured wrapping paper, ribbon bows, and a babble of laughter and delighted voices. Jennifer's hand closed on the square package from Logan to her. After a brief flare of curiosity, she buried it beneath another from Sheila.

'Oh, Jenny, thank you!' Mrs. Taylor exclaimed exuberantly, her fingers caressed the book fondly 'Someone must have told you of my obsession for books.'

'Yes, they did,' Jennifer admitted.

Then Jennifer's attention was drawn by the excited voice of her sister. She was holding aloft a beautiful turquoise and silver necklace.

'It's magnificent, Logan,' Sheila breathed softly, as she hurriedly clasped it around her neck and lovingly fingered the delicately stamped silver chain.

Logan was gazing at her with undisguised tenderness and admiration. 'The Navajo Indians believe that happiness and good fortune come to all who wear the turquoise stone. I hope you'll wear it as a symbol of all the things I wish for you.'

Embarrassed to be unwillingly listening to Logan's declaration, Jennifer turned frustratedly to his mother, hoping to relieve the pain that was now gnawing at her breast. Mrs. Taylor was gazing at her son with a light of dawning wonder in her eyes. Quickly she glanced at Jennifer with the most absurdly bright twinkle in her eyes and a tremulous smile of pleasure on her lips. Jennifer suddenly realized that there was some significance to the necklace that Sheila had received. That smile on Mrs. Taylor's face had a knowing look to it that had nothing to do with the mere exchanging of Christmas gifts.

Jennifer felt suddenly confused and helpless. Things were happening too quickly for her to have any control in shaping her own plans. She turned to Dirk, whose mouth had twisted into a grim line as he left the couch to help Cindy assemble one of her toys. He had noticed it, too. What was she going to do? she thought as her hands fumbled with a package.

Logan slid silently into the seat beside Jennifer so recently vacated by Dirk. In his hands was her present to him, still wrapped.

'As big and heavy as this is, I wonder if I should dare open it,' he mocked her.

All of the impish pleasure that she had known when she had purchased his present was gone. She would have given anything to be able to snatch it away from his hands. But there he was busily unwrapping the paper. It was only a matter of seconds before the contents were revealed to Logan. Jennifer nearly cringed, awaiting his reaction, feeling none of the malicious amusement she had anticipated. After staring at it almost increduously, Logan threw his head back and roared with laughter. Every person in the room turned their attention to him as Jennifer coloured furiously beneath his laughing eyes.

He tore away the rest of the paper to show everyone the large basket of fruit. Since no one else had taken part in their conversation that day of the sleigh ride, they did not see the humour of the gift and stared in puzzlement at Logan.

'Only you would think of this, Jenny Glenn.' Deep amusement rimmed his every word as his gaze shifted from her to his mother. 'I once told Jenny of my habit of sampling different "fruit",' he explained, 'so here we have everything from oranges to the proverbial apple of temptation.'

Mrs. Taylor's melodic laugh joined in with the more hesitant ones from the rest of the group. Gradually everyone's attention was diverted back to their own gifts, allowing Jennifer's complexion to return to its normal colour. After unwrapping her present from Dirk and inhaling the scent of the expensive perfume, she was left with only one package, Logan's. She was reluctant to open it with him sitting right beside her. At that moment Sheila enlisted his help in the kitchen and Jennifer was able to open it without his embarrassing presence.

A black, rectangular jewellery case gleamed out to her from the partially removed paper. Cautiously she opened it and barely stifled a gasp of surprise and pleasure at its contents. On a cushion of white velvet rested two strands of delicate gold chain holding a cabochon-cut jade stone encircled by antique filigree work with brilliants of diamonds dotting the corners. She didn't know too much about gems, but this was obviously a very expensive piece of jewellery. She closed the lid quickly on the exquisite work of art, knowing she should refuse it yet longing to see it around her neck.

'Jenny, would you give me a hand with the eggnog?' Sheila requested as she passed a tray to Mrs. Taylor, oblivious of the stunned silence of her sister.

'Of course.' Jennifer was all too glad to put Logan's

present down. Her hand was practically on fire just touching it.

She escaped as quickly as she could into the kitchen, avoiding any contact with Logan's searching eyes as she darted past him. But minutes later, his footsteps muffled by the clinking of crystal glasses, he entered the kitchen.

'Sheila makes awfully good eggnog,' he remarked as he halted beside her.

Jennifer's hand paused midway between filling another glass. She tried to breathe naturally while smiling an agreement with him.

'You're not wearing the necklace,' glancing casually at her unadorned neck. 'I thought it would look nice with that gown.'

Jennifer placed the ladle back in the bowl and turned towards him with a determined lift to her chin.

'It was very beautiful,' she said sincerely, 'but I just can't accept it.'

He lifted an eyebrow at her as the small smile died on his face. 'Why not?'

'It's much too expensive.' She suddenly found it difficult to explain why she wanted to refuse it. 'It just wouldn't be right for me to.'

'We can hardly be considered strangers—after all, we spent a night together in the same bed. I would hardly think a piece of costume jewellery could be classified as a compromising gift after that.'

'Costume jewellery?' Jennifer whispered in an astounded voice. 'I thought it was jade.'

'It's jadeite,' Logan informed her with a dimpling

106

smile.

'Oh!' Her voice sounded exceedingly small. That must be some synthetic form of jade, she thought. How humiliating for her to believe he was giving her an expensive gift. 'Well, in that case, I guess it will be all right to accept it.'

'I'm glad. After all, I accepted your gift in the spirit it was intended.' His teasing voice brought a fresh wave of pink into her cheeks, only to recede quickly to paleness as he continued, 'Sheila told me you were the one who invited Dirk here tonight.'

'Yes, that's right.'

'I didn't realize that in the short space of a week you and Dirk had become such close friends.'

'I don't know that we're close friends.' Jennifer answered him casually, but there was a defiant gleam in her eyes. 'Both of us have a very deep affection for my sister. I think Dirk would make an excellent husband and father.'

'You do? You've taken matters in your own hands and decided you know what's best for your sister's future happiness.' He was again wearing his mask of amused indifference that was so irritatingly smug. 'I hope you don't try the direct approach. I've found subtlety works best with Sheila. I do agree with you on one point—I think it's time she remarried.'

His words hung in the air as if his sentence was unfinished. Mentally Jennifer finished it for him, 'but not to Dirk.' To Logan?

'Are you going to try to stop Dirk and me?' She tilted her head back to glare coldly into his face.

'I would never stand in the way of Sheila's happiness. But that's Sheila's decision, not yours or mine, Jenny Glenn.' A roguish dimple appeared briefly in one cheek as Logan answered with a remarkable air of assurance. He reached around her and picked up a tray of glasses filled with eggnog. 'I'll take these in before they send a search party for us.'

Jennifer stared after him blankly, a sinking feeling of depression stealing through her, as he walked out of the kitchen. She was sure that Dirk loved her sister very deeply. But could Logan's love be even greater since he had practically said he was willing to step aside if it meant Sheila's happiness? Just the thought made her heart constrict painfully until her hand reached up to clutch her dress and thus tear away the ache. A vision of Logan and Sheila in an embrace flitted across her mind, sending waves of nausea to her stomach.

Too late Jennifer recognized the true reason behind her betrayal of her sister to Dirk's side. She had fallen in love with Logan Taylor herself! For her it had gone much deeper than a mere physical attraction such as Logan had once suggested. No, not when she could be shaken to her very bones with jealousy towards her own sister and this heart-rending pain at the discovery that Logan loved Sheila to the exclusion of his own happiness. Could she be as unselfish as Logan? Jennifer wondered, blinking at the tears that were threatening to overflow down her cheeks. One thing was certain—she must never let Sheila Logan know her true feelings.

The rest of the evening would be her first test. Dipping down into her now almost depleted reserve of willpower, Jennifer inhaled deeply, fixed a smile on her face, and began the long walk into the living room, determined that no one would know the secret that haunted the depths of her soul.

# CHAPTER SEVEN

JENNIFER had made it through Christmas Eve and Christmas and the four days that followed them, but the morning of the fifth day seemed to bring with it a prediction of all the days to come.

The holiday vacation had brought with it an increase in guests taking advantage of their free time to indulge in the facilities at the ski slopes. Logan had been ever-present at the Lodge, never usurping Sheila's position as manager, only assisting to ease her workload. Jennifer had taken precautions to avoid being near him whenever possible, hiding in Dirk's shadow, if he was available, trying to erect a barrier against Logan's magnetism. But she couldn't cease the fluttering of her heart when his gaze rested on her, nor could she wash away the acrid taste of jealousy from her mouth when she saw him with Sheila.

Oh, she had erected a very elaborate façade of gaiety, but she knew exactly how brittle it was, and how easily it could be shattered. The arrival of DeeDee Hunter, the platinum blonde Jennifer had met at the airport with Logan, had very nearly put a crack in it this very morning. Just watching the mild flirting between Dee-Dee and Logan had filled her with a mixture of envy and jealousy. If only she could meet his eyes as easily as DeeDee and feel the warmth of his virility directed at her! But she couldn't. Jennifer had too much pride to hang on his arm as others did, grateful for whatever crumbs were thrown her way, nor would she compete with her own sister who had known so much heartache in her short life.

At last, Jennifer's afternoon replacement arrived, and she was freed of her front desk duties to go home. Quickly she shrugged into her suede coat, conscious of the giggling voice of DeeDee Hunter approaching the lobby. Her sixth sense told her that Logan was most probably with her. She hurried across the lobby, seeing with a sinking heart the airport limousine unloading at the front door. Glancing over her shoulder, she saw Logan stop with DeeDee and two others from her party, at the front desk. Jennifer stood at the front door, tapping her foot impatiently, nodding and smiling to the new arrivals as they filed through. One of them stopped suddenly in front of her. His face gradually separated itself from the rest of the strangers as the familiarness registered.

'Jennifer?'

She stared numbly into a pair of dark eyes, blinking disbelievingly back at her before two hands reached out to imprison her shoulders. A black lock of hair fell forward across his forehead.

'Jennifer! I can't believe it's really you!'

'Brad,' Jennifer finally whispered increduously. 'What are you doing here?'

'What are you doing here?' he laughed. His grasp tightened momentarily on her shoulders as if to draw her into his arms, before his expression sobered. 'You don't know what hell I've put myself through wondering where you were, if you were all right. And then fate sends you right in front of me!'

'How did you know I was here?' Her lips were compressed in a forbidding line, her eyes burning with an angry fire at the almost forgotten humiliation she had suffered in this man's hands.

'I didn't know! I wanted to get away. It was a last-minute decision, and since I couldn't get reservations anywhere in Colorado, I came here,' he replied in that familiar flattering tone. 'Don't look at me like that, Jennifer. I know what happened was practically unforgivable.'

'I don't want to talk about it.' Jennifer twisted out of his arms, her scowling face glancing up just in time to see Logan walking towards them.

'You're wrong. We've got a lot to talk about,' Brad replied firmly.

'Excuse me.' Logan glanced politely at Brad before addressing himself to Jennifer. 'Your sister wondered if you would pick up the children for her. She can't get away right now.'

'Of course,' Jennifer nodded, feeling the blood rush out of her cheeks under his sardonic gaze.

Logan looked expectantly towards Brad, then back to Jennifer, anticipating an introduction that Jennifer was loath to make. But one look at his determined expression told her that if she didn't, he would.

'This is Mr. Taylor, Brad, the owner of this Lodge.' Jennifer barely suppressed her irritation from creeping into her words. 'Bradley Stevenson, a friend from Minneapolis.'

Brad accepted Logan's handshake, hiding his impatience with professional politeness.

'We're glad to have one of Jenny's friend's staying at our lodge,' Logan said smoothly. 'How long did you plan to be here?'

'Only three days. I'll have to leave on Sunday's flight. I hope to see as much of Jennifer as possible while I'm here. Since you're her employer now, I might as well forewarn you that I'm going to do everything in my power to persuade her to return with me and take her old job back.'

Jennifer's eyes flew to Brad in alarm at the same moment that Logan's voice rang out with deceptive curiosity.

'Old job?'

'Yes, Jennifer was my secretary as well as,' Brad hesitated suggestively, eyeing her warmly, 'other things.'

Logan's eyes narrowed as he studied her flushed cheeks below downcast eyes.

'It's unfortunate that Jenny didn't tell me you were coming.' He didn't hide the arrogance and censure in his voice. 'I could possibly have arranged for her to have some free time. But this is the height of our season. As it stands it's quite impossible to spare her.'

'I understand,' Brad drawled, meeting the challenge of Logan's gaze with his usual self-confidence. His hand reached out for Jennifer's arm and he pulled her possessively to his side. 'Now, if you'll excuse us?'

Logan nodded a silent agreement, his penetrating gaze resting briefly on Jennifer before he walked away.

'Let's go somewhere where we can talk,' Brad suggested the minute Logan was out of hearing.

'I-I can't. I have to pick up the children.' Jennifer stalled. 'And Sheila won't be home until late tonight, which means I'll have to babysit.'

'I'll come over to the house, then.'

'No!' Her reply was quick and sharp, but she qualified it in a quieter voice. 'Two children hardly allow for any private discussions.'

'Tomorrow, then.'

'I'll be working.'

'Jennifer, I'm going to talk to you alone. You are not going to think up a bunch of excuses to avoid me while I'm here. You have got to give me a chance to explain,' Brad argued. 'After that—well, if you don't want to see me, I won't bother you.'

'All right,' Jennifer sighed. Who would have thought a month ago that she could be so indifferent to Brad today? At this moment she didn't care if she never saw him again. 'Tomorrow night the Lodge is giving a New Year's Eve party. As Sheila's sister and an employee, I have to attend, but I'm sure that later in the evening I can spend some time with you.'

'You'll be glad you did.' Brad gazed down at her with that winning smile that used to enchant her so.

'I have to go now,' she replied, completely unmoved by his attempt.

'Till tomorrow,' he agreed softly, bending his head to touch his lips to her forehead. They felt cold to her skin

114

and she barely repressed a shudder as she hurried out the Lodge door.

'Are you going to lunch now, Jenny?' the plump-figured switchboard operator asked.

'Uhuh,' Jennifer confirmed, kneeling down to take her bag out of one of the drawers and discreetly apply a fresh touch of lipstick to her lips. 'Just a quick bite. I won't be long.'

'I bet!' Carol exclaimed with a short laugh.

'What's that supposed to mean?' Jennifer gazed curiously at the smug expression on her working partner's face.

'Listen, if I was having lunch with a dream of a guy, you can bet it would take me an hour just to eat the salad!'

'What are you talking about?'

'Before you came on duty this morning, this gorgeous hunk of a man stopped at the desk and asked what time you went to lunch. and I told him,' Carol replied, tilting her brown head to the side at Jennifer's blankness. 'You met him yesterday when he arrived from the airport. I assumed you were having lunch with him, aren't you?'

'No,' answered Jennifer, shaking her head in puzzlement. Brad hadn't mentioned anything about lunch.

'You just didn't think you were,' the other girl teased. 'Boy, you are really lucky having a handsome man like that in your pocket.'

'Handsome is as handsome does,' Jennifer retorted. 'Don't let the good looks fool you, Carol. In some cases, it really is only skin deep.'

115

'If I had somebody like that, he could use me as a doormat any time he wanted,' Carol asserted, rolling her eyes expressively.

'Tell me that after some guy has wiped his feet on you,' Jennifer responded.

'Talking about Apollo——' Carol gestured sideways with her head towards the man approaching the counter.

'Hey, Jennifer. How about lunch with me before I hit the ski slopes?' Brad suggested gaily. His gaze roved admiringly over Jennifer's grey and black plaid skirt with its matching black jacket.

'Brad, I——'

'I'm sorry, Jenny won't be able to,' Logan interrupted. She turned in surprise. With his catlike quietness she hadn't heard him walk up.

'Why not?' Brad's face was mottled with disbelief.

'It's a policy of the Lodge that guests and employees don't socialize in public,' Logan stated firmly. 'Whatever company you and Miss Glenn keep will have to be after she's off work.'

'What's the harm in two people eating a sandwich together?' Brad retorted argumentatively. 'Surely this is a special case. I've travelled clear from Minneapolis, and I'm leaving in two days!'

'There's a table reserved especially for the staff which assures them prompt service and prevents the problem of tardiness. As to making an exception,' Logan glanced cynically at the growing indignation on Jennifer's face before smiling regretfully at Brad, 'I just don't see how I could do it. I'm sure any case

116

would be a special case in the eyes of the person requesting it.'

'And that's your final word?' Brad asked, shoving a clenched fist in the pocket of his blue ski jacket.

'Yes, it is. Now if you'll excuse me, I have some business to attend to.'

With a condescending nod to each of them, Logan returned to the private offices behind the reception area. Jennifer exchanged a puzzled glance with Carol before turning, astounded and angry, back to Brad.

'He's got to be one of the most pompous, dominating——' His eyes burned with a black flame as he stared at Jennifer.

'I agree,' she interrupted, 'but it's the policy just the same. It's just as well. I only have time for a quick lunch anyway. I'll see you tonight, Brad.'

'Right, and with no intrusions from him!' he snapped loudly before stalking angrily out of the lobby.

'What was all that about?' Carol whispered as she glanced fearfully towards the offices in case Logan should pounce out at them again. 'I've never heard any objections raised before about the staff eating with a guest. We usually just invite them to the staff table.'

'I know.' Jennifer's lips were pressed firmly together. 'I think I was just made the exception, and I'd certainly like to know why!'

'Are you going to ask him?' Carol breathed in astonishment.

Jennifer hesitated. She had no inclination to see Logan alone, but still.... 'If the opportunity arises,' she answered. 'First I'm going to lunch.'

Jennifer gazed around the throng of holidaymakers, some donning gaily festooned caps to emphasize their high spirits. The small combo in the far corner of the room blared forth a popular tune as couples crowded on to the floor, laughing and shouting at one another, caring nothing about the melody, only that it was in rhythm with their bounding spirits. It was strictly an informal affair with dress varying from ski outfits to cocktail dresses and dark suits and ties. Her own dress fell somewhere in between, with its simple lines of white chiffon fitting the bodice tightly while the skirt of accordion pleats curled at the hem, lending it an air of ethereal innocence. The jade necklace around her neck glittered brightly against the white dress.

The clinking of ice brought Jennifer's attention around to the dark-haired man holding out a glass to her. She smiled her thanks to Brad as she accepted the drink. He had set himself out to be as charming and urbane as possible, the personification of politeness and solicitude. He had rarely left her side the entire evening, although she was amused by his straying glances at the younger, more attractive females at the party. Although there had been several opportunities for them to slip away, Jennifer was grateful that Brad hadn't pushed the point. She needed to be surrounded by the noise and gaiety, to take refuge in the merry revelry. Her eyes trailed over the crowd, seeking out Logan and finding him amidst a group of DeeDee's party. He was listening attentively to the vibrant blonde, yet he seemed to be holding himself apart from them. 'Suffering their attentions with that lordly air of his,' Jennifer thought cynically. That was a totally unfair remark, she chided herself. What did she expect him to do?

Her eyes misted brightly with pain as she watched her sister make her way towards Logan, touch his arm, and become the recipient of his warm regard. Sheila was breathtakingly lovely tonight in a dress of burgundy red velvet with her raven hair in ringlets of sophisticated curls atop her head. Their discussion was brief as Sheila nodded agreement with something Logan had said before walking away. Jennifer's heart ached painfully at his lingering glance on her sister's retreating form.

Brad touched her elbow, tearing her attention away from the scene, and suggested that they dance. She let herself be swept into the pulsating dancers, willing the music to drown out her thoughts. Later as a dreamy ballad echoed through the room, Jennifer clung tightly to Brad. Her eyes closed, her senses unaware of the way her fingers curved tenaciously into his shoulder, while her head rested lightly against his chest. Brad's steps stopped suddenly, and Jennifer's head moved away from its comfortable place as she stared blankly into Logan's sardonic face.

'No objection to an employer cutting in, is there?' His eyebrow raised over a cynically questioning eye.

Brad grimly consented and stepped away from his stunned companion. Jennifer stiffened as Logan's hand touched her waist. She held herself apart from him, her hand resting tensely against his shoulder while the other was captured in his firm grip. Her feet became incredibly awkward as she stumbled to follow his simple steps. She found she could look anywhere but into his face.

'If you can't relax, we might as well sit this one out,' Logan said sharply.

'Duty dances never were my line,' Jennifer managed to retort sarcastically, aware that her cheeks were flushed and her heart was beating at an erratic pace.

'I'm beginning to wonder just exactly what your "line" is.' Logan's hand gripped her elbow determinedly as he manoeuvred her off the floor towards a dark, uninhabited corner of the room.

'What about you and your edict about guests and employees?' she asked scathingly, secretly knowing her barbed words could never inflict the pain and heartbreak on him that she was feeling.

'I was under the impression that you wouldn't want the presence of the man you *said* had made unwelcome advances. It seems you have forgiven him.' Jennifer was surprised that Logan's face could have such an aura of savage ruthlessness about it.

'I've forgiven him,' she murmured. Of course, she'd forgiven him because she didn't care any more. He didn't matter to her, but how could she possibly tell Logan that?

'How gracious of you!' Logan removed a cigarette from his jacket pocket and snapped a gold lighter to it angrily. 'Does that mean you'll be leaving on Sunday?'

'No, it doesn't,' Jennifer replied sharply.

'Surely that would make the reconciliation complete?'

'There hasn't been one yet. And if there is——'
Jennifer paused. Her mind raced over the possibility.
Could she dare wrap herself in the deception of a
relationship with Brad? Would it cloak her with an
armour to protect her from Logan? One thing was
certain, if she didn't close the door with Brad, at least
in everyone else's eyes, she would have a perfect alibi
for leaving when the time came for her to go. 'If there
is, I wouldn't leave right away. I wouldn't want to be
swept away by my emotions. I'd want time to think
about it. Plus, I wouldn't want Sheila to be caught in
the lurch by my desertion.'

'It's amazing how a woman can be so cold-blooded
and analytical in the face of a powerful emotion like
love. Aren't you tempting fate by withholding such a
morsel?' His eyes raked her body thoroughly, sending
a wave of colour into her cheeks. 'What if he finds
some one else who isn't as coolheaded as you?'

'I'll take my chances,' she replied evenly.

'You can't possibly be in love with him! There
would be nothing to think about. You don't even know
what love is!' Her heart and lungs came screeching to
a halt as Logan's hand forced her chin upwards before
she could twist away. There was no masking the anger
and contempt in his eyes. 'Enjoy your victory in bringing him to heel. But you are not going to marry him!'

'Why, you pompous, interfering . . .! I'm not Sheila,
Logan Taylor! And I'm not going to allow you to run
my life!' Jennifer exclaimed angrily, even though deep
in her heart, she knew without him she would have no
life, only an existence.

'You are not going to marry him,' Logan said firmly, calmly and coldly.

'It's none of your business what I do.' Even to her own ears the words sounded weak and ineffectual, but it didn't matter. Logan wasn't there to hear them. He was already mixing with a group of laughing people on the side of the dance floor.

Silently she watched him, her eyes smarting with unshed tears. She saw him stop beside Sheila before encircling her sister's waist with one arm and whisk her out on the dance floor, an enchanting warm smile on his face as he gazed down at her. Jennifer felt as if she was stepping off the lowest rung on the ladder.

'I've asked her to dance three times, and she's refused *me* every time.' Dirk spoke up from Jennifer's side.

She turned a pair of startled eyes on him, believing herself alone in the wasteland of merrymakers. His bleak, gloomy expression matched hers as they stared together at the dancing couple.

'I can't even ask "How are you?", but what she doesn't get that chilly expression on her face that says she'd like to turn me into a snowman,' Dirk grumbled. running a hand through his dark hair dejectedly.

'I think the secret is don't ask,' Jennifer sighed. She glanced at him sadly. Too many times she had seen Logan and Dirk standing side by side and Dirk always came out second best. She sympathized with his futility at competing with Logan Taylor. 'Why don't you go cut in on them?' she suggested softly.

'After all, Sheila's not about to make a scene in the middle of the floor.'

It would be a small victory for Dirk, Jennifer thought, but in the end he would pay the same price as she, when Sheila walked down the aisle to Logan. All the little battles and skirmishes would not change the final outcome, and Logan would be the victor.

Jennifer watched as Logan relinquished his partner to Dirk, his eyes gleaming in triumphant hope, but she turned away before Logan's searching eyes could possibly meet hers. Brad would be looking for her by now. She derived solace from that thought. Without him as a crutch this evening, she would have turned tail and run. Slowly, she made her way through the crowd until she could see his dark head bending courteously towards one of the older people in the group. When he finally saw her, his dark eyes sparkled brightly at her.

'Jennifer.' He reached out a hand and drew her into the circle of his arm. He nuzzled her red-gold hair for a brief moment before excusing himself from the group. 'It's almost the witching hour. Can't we bring in the New Year alone?'

Why not? she thought to herself. The laughter, the music, the noise, were all compounding the strain of the evening. She made no protest as Brad led her out of the room down a vacant hallway.

'Do you have any idea how much I wanted to be alone with you all evening?' Brad murmured, imprisoning her against the wall with his arms.

'Please, Brad, don't,' Jennifer protested as he sought

123

to take her in his arms.

'I don't blame you for pushing me away.' Brad's hand caressed her cheek lightly. 'What I did that night was unforgivable—I know that. Can't you give me a chance to make it up to you?' Jennifer turned her face away from him, fighting the nausea of the memory and the odour of alcohol on his breath now. He removed his hand from her cheek, his pleading eyes searching her face. 'I was drunk and angry that night. I admit that you were nothing more to me than another girl. I told myself I was glad that you'd gone, that there were plenty more where you came from. Then you began to haunt me. No matter what I did, or where I went, I couldn't get you out of my mind. Come back with me.'

'Brad, it's over and done with,' Jennifer sighed. 'There's no way back.'

'Don't you see, Jennifer? It was your innocence and purity that aroused me.' His voice was hoarse.

Where had she heard that before? Jennifer thought in defeat.

'I wanted you then, and, God help me, I still want you now.'

'You don't love me, Brad,' calmly. 'I aroused your desire, but I never touched your heart. Be honest with yourself. If you hadn't run into me here by accident, in a month you would have forgotten me completely.'

'That's not true,' Brad whispered, gathering her into his arms. 'I'll prove it to you, that it's not true.'

His lips descended passionately on hers. Indifference would more effectively check his ardour than resistence, so Jennifer remained passive in his arms, her lips remaining cool to his kiss. Distantly she heard the chant of the New Year's celebrants as they counted down the seconds of the old year before they broke loose in a chorus of jubilant Happy New Years to the melancholy strains of 'Auld Lang Syne'. She closed her eyes tightly to prevent the tears from falling, indifferent to the fact that Brad's mouth had deserted her lips to rain kisses on her neck.

Was this a portent of the year to come? she wondered. Here, in the arms of a man who meant nothing to her, who could never mean anything to her? 'Should auld acquaintance be forgot and never brought to mind?' The words tore at her heart as Logan's image drifted clearly into her mind. No, she thought cynically, there was no chance that she would ever forget him.

Her eyes opened to look out through the mist of tears. Slowly her vision cleared, and she became aware of a figure in the hallway. Her heart sank as she looked over Brad's shoulder into Logan's glaring eyes. For one brief moment their eyes were locked before he turned on his heel and walked stiffly away.

## CHAPTER EIGHT

It lacked three days from being a month since Brad, after another evening of persistent persuasion at dinner and later dancing, had finally realized that Jennifer plainly wasn't interested in him any more and had taken his scheduled flight back to Minneapolis.

Of course, Jennifer never related any of this to anyone, even though Sheila had been quite determined to find out the results. But Jennifer just allowed her and anyone else to believe that she was considering Brad's offer. It was remarkably easy, she discovered, since everyone thought it was so romantic that Brad would have come all this way just to see her, which should surely prove he loved her. And it suited her purpose not to let them find out that he had had no idea that she was even here. A non-existent lover in a faraway town was a salve to her pride that chided her for falling so irrevocably in love with Logan Taylor.

She had tried desperately to replace that emotion with hatred and distaste, but only succeeded in generating occasional sparks of anger. The brief flare-ups had been worthless as Logan wasn't around to be a part of them. He seemed to be avoiding her as much as she was avoiding him. That wasn't quite true. He had been absent a great deal, but he had had very good reason.

There had been numerous stockmen's warnings this last month when winter had descended on the mountains with a fury. His presence at the ranch had been required a great deal of the time.

The holiday season had passed, and the skiers were coming now only on the weekends. Carol was perfectly capable of handling the switchboard and the tours and the front desk duties, with Sheila pitching in if there was an abnormal rush. Jennifer was back to spending the weekdays at the house and helping out at the Lodge on the weekends if the reservations were heavy.

Dependable, determined Dirk was still banging his head away at Sheila's stone wall, making little progress. Although once in a while Jennifer noted the mortar chipping, Sheila quickly patched it up.

Jennifer knew why she was still staying here at Jackson, and Dirk was the reason. If by some wild, unimaginable chance he could succeed in capturing Sheila, though the possibility seemed terribly remote, Logan would be free. She just wished there was some way she could help Dirk, but her sister was very adept at making sure that Dirk never got very close to her.

'It's no use,' Jennifer thought. Not even this morning's excursion of window shopping through the town had managed to get her mind off the situation. At least, lunching with her sister would ensure that none of the things that were occupying Jennifer's mind would be aired openly. She sighed wearily as she pushed open the Lodge door and fixed a cheery smile on her face as she greeted Carol.

'Is Sheila busy?'

'I don't think so,' Carol shrugged. 'She's back in the office. Go on in.'

Jennifer nodded, opening the counter gate and proceeding down the small hallway behind the reception area to the private offices. She rapped lightly on Sheila's door before opening it. She poked her head around the door, expecting to see her sister's raven head bent over her desk, but the room was empty. Her eyebrows drew together in a frown as she closed the door quietly. She started to return to the reception desk when she heard Sheila's voice coming from an adjacent office.

'Why must you keep dragging him into our conversations!'

'Because you take such pains to keep him out.' That was Logan. Jennifer hadn't realized he was back in town.

'I've told you Dirk means nothing to me!' Sheila was asserting vehemently.

'Then why can't you discuss him rationally without panicking into hysteria? I get the feeling you're protesting too much.'

'Don't be ridiculous!'

'I'm not the one who's being ridiculous.' Jennifer heard a movement of someone getting out of a chair and then footsteps as Logan paused before continuing. 'I want you to be sure, Sheila, very sure. Don't turn him into a ghost that will haunt you for the rest of your life with "what-might-have-been".'

'Can't you take my word for it, that he means nothing to me?' Sheila's voice was strained as if she was holding back tears.

'No, I can't,' Logan replied grimly. 'You're going to have to prove it to me.'

'What more can I say? What more can I do?'

'You can stop avoiding him. If he invites you out, go with him. If what you once felt is really and truly gone, then he'll be out of your system once and for all.'

'I couldn't do that.'

'Do it for me, Sheila.'

'Logan, I. . . .'

Whatever statement Sheila was about to make was muffled, and Jennifer knew instinctively it was because Logan had taken her in his arms. She managed to tiptoe back to the front desk, the pain tearing at her throat as she tried to swallow her sobs. Somehow she was able to tell Carol that Sheila was busy, and that she was going on home, barely making it out the door before the tears started streaming down her cheeks. She was crying not just for herself, but for Logan, too, who was forcing the woman he loved into the company of her former lover so that when she came to him there would be no ghosts to haunt their love.

'Jenny! Jennifer!' a voice called out as she tried to dash past the stocky figure approaching the Lodge. His hand caught and held her arm while she wiped desperately at her tears with her free hand.

'Hey, what's this all about?' Dirk brushed a sparkling tear away.

Jennifer shrugged her shoulders, pressing her lips together to stem the flow of pain from her chest. She inhaled deeply before lifting her head to smile tremulously at him.

'A silly feminine trait, I guess, crying for no reason at all.'

'I've seen that look of misery in your eyes before,' wryly, 'when you thought no one else was looking, and your mask slipped out of place.' His arm reached out, encircling her shoulders to draw her comfortably against his side. 'Why don't you tell Uncle Dirk all about it?'

'There's nothing to tell.' Jennifer hoped she had a convincing lilt to her voice.

'Come on now.' Cajoling he squeezed her shoulders. 'You've been depressed ever since your beau from Minnesota left.'

'I suppose I have.'

'I was just going into the Lodge for a sandwich and some soup. If you don't feel like eating, then come and sympathize with me over a cup of coffee,' Dirk insisted firmly.

Jennifer glanced reluctantly towards the Lodge. Logan was there. So what? she told herself defiantly. Was she going to let him rule her life, dictating the places where she could and could not go?

'Sounds good,' she agreed quickly.

He didn't allow her an opportunity to change her mind, but led her directly into the Lodge, through the lobby, and into the café. Once there, he ordered for himself and at the same time directed the waitress to bring Jennifer a small bowl of chilli. 'To stoke her furnace,' he told her in an aside. From there on he took charge of the conversation. His banter, light-hearted and removed from any serious discussions, slowly soothed her jangled nerves until Jennifer was able to take part with more of her usual high spirits than she had managed to summon in the past few weeks.

She was laughing easily over an anecdote that Dirk had related to her about an Art Nouveau exhibit, when she found herself looking into Logan's narrowed eyes as he gazed at them from the café entrance. Though her heart leaped to her throat, choking her laughter off momentarily, she managed to turn her now over-bright eyes back to Dirk, conscious that every step Logan was taking was bringing him closer to their table.

Polite greetings were exchanged when Logan finally reached them. He declined Dirk's courteous invitation to join them.

'It's quite a coincidence finding the two of you here together,' Logan smiled, but the smile failed to relieve the penetrating harshness of his eyes. 'Sheila and I were just discussing the fact that Jenny hadn't had a chance to see the Grand Tetons. I suggested that next week the four of us make a day of it.'

Dirk's expression was as cynical as Jennifer's, though he agreed quickly to the suggestion. Jennifer stared at the table, silently applauding with bitterness Logan's manipulations that enabled Sheila to be in Dirk's company even if under Logan's chaperonage.

'What do you say, Jenny?' Logan's hardening gaze studied her intently.

131

She longed to tell him haughtily that the last thing she wanted was to spend a day in his company, as an unwelcome fourth at that. But even before her head began to nod her assent, Jennifer knew she would never say it. Like a lamb being led to slaughter, she bowed her head to fate.

'I'll check with the weather bureau to see which day promises to be clear, and let you know.' His smile was sardonic at Jennifer's indifferent agreement.

'You don't seem overjoyed with the suggestion.' Dirk studied her keenly as her haunted eyes followed the retreating figure of Logan Taylor.

What could she say, Jennifer thought—that she didn't like being used as a pawn in one of Logan's calculated moves to capture the queen? No, she couldn't tell Dirk the real reason behind Logan's invitation. She knew his heart leaped at the idea of spending a day in Sheila's company, whereas her own had taken a nosedive.

'Probably because he was so arrogantly sure we would agree,' she finally replied.

'Which we did.' His expression was thoughtful as he eyed the defiant set of her chin and the rueful gleam in her eyes. 'I wonder if you agreed for the same reason as I did?'

She didn't reply to the question, knowing that Dirk would astutely see through any lie.

'I'm sure we'll have a lovely time.' She sighed instead, fully aware there was a great deal of bitterness and self-pity contained in that sigh.

The brilliance of the mid-morning sun intensified the stark whiteness of the snow as the four walked slowly under the snow-covered, roofed archway towards the log chapel. Its simple wood cross on the roof peak was edged with snow.

The rustic humbleness of the church increased Jennifer's feeling of infinite sanctity, this tiny house of God meekly surrounded by mountain cathedrals.

Logan held the door open as they entered the chapel. The unpretentious wooden floor and log-covered walls with simple log and slat pews modestly welcomed them. No one needed to be reminded that this was a place of worship for all eyes were drawn to the altar. A simple cross of wood stood silhouetted against the altar window, framing the distant Teton peaks, their white spiralling heads against the vividly blue sky. The enveloping awe touched Jennifer with the omnipotence of God as she stared at the glory of God's own work, majestic and incapable of being equalled by man's hands.

It was such a clear reminder of the mightiness of her Creator that Jennifer's eyes smarted with tears at the holiness of the simple chapel. Pictures of all the grandiose churches that had been built as palatial temples of worship suddenly seemed to be overstated. The opulence of those buildings could never match the spiritual peace and tranquillity within these plain wood walls and the ethereal splendour of God's mountains behind the simple wood cross and altar.

Several minutes later, with their silence never broken, Logan and Sheila, Jennifer and Dirk filed out of the church.

'The Chapel of the Transfiguration,' Jennifer whispered reverently, once outside. 'I thought it was such a peculiar name. But now. . . .'

The unfinished sentence needed no explanation.

'It's so perfect.' She searched inadequately for the words again as she turned towards Logan. 'Who? How?'

'A family from California who spent several summers here were mainly responsible for raising the money to build it.' He smiled his agreement with speechlessness. 'It was built in 1925, an Episcopal church, but open to all faiths. Although we've barely entered the Park, I couldn't think of a better way to start our tour.'

'Neither could I!' Jennifer agreed.

Their short conversation had separated them from Sheila and Dirk, who had already reached the jeep. It was as if a truce had now been called between the warring parties. Everyone had gained peace in those few minutes spent inside the chapel.

'Over there is the Maude Noble Cabin.' Logan gestured towards the building opposite the Chapel. 'That's where the meeting was held that led to the establishment of the Grand Teton National Park. To the north is the Bill Menor Cabin. He was the first settler west of the Snake River and operated a ferry for over twenty-five years here. I'm afraid there's too much to see and do, for us to do more than skim the top. The Park roads are closed in the winter, so we'll have to give you the highlights via the highway running through it.'

'I don't mind. Perhaps there'll be another time.' A wistfulness coloured her words, knowing she wouldn't be there long enough to see the mountains in their summer dress.

'There will be, Jenny.'

There was such a marked degree of certainty in his voice that Jennifer raised her head to look at him, but they had already reached their vehicle and Logan was holding the rear door open for her. His gaze was soft as it rested briefly on her face, yet there was nothing there to reveal that his comment held any special meaning.

Once again they were all back in the jeep, Sheila safely in front with Logan, Jennifer behind with Dirk. But the strain that had been evident in the foursome was gone, and Jennifer knew the rest of the trip would be made in this companionable air of mutual enjoyment.

Back on the main road, Logan pointed out the wooded mesa called Blacktail Butte, named for the large number of blacktail or mule deer that were formerly found in the area. They travelled slowly, pausing along the roadside to watch an occasional moose grazing among the bushes and trees of the Snake River that coiled and uncoiled between the highway and the mountains. The austere grandeur of the craggy peaks decked out in winter splendour were presented in ever-changing views. Wispy trails of blowing snow danced down a slope, flirting in crevices before fading into stillness where the wind died. The cottonwoods along the riverbank and the aspens sprinkled through the slopes were dressed in shimmering ice while the pines wore garlands of snow. The scenes were sometimes ethereal in their beauty, sometimes majestic and imposing, but Jennifer's eyes were always drawn to the towering mountains.

At last Logan pulled to the side of the road and turned off the motor.

'Snake River Overlook,' he announced, glancing back at Jennifer before getting out of the jeep to open her door.

Jennifer stood quietly at his side to wait for Shelia and Dirk to join them. But Logan took her elbow and guided her across the road without waiting for the other pair. For one unwelcome moment she was reminded of the real reason for this trip, so Sheila could be with Dirk. Quickly, Jennifer shoved the thought aside. It was a perfect day, and she wasn't going to allow anything to spoil it. Still she couldn't prevent herself from glancing over her shoulder at her sister, who looked like a fashion model in black ski pants and black parka, trimmed in white fur with a white hood that framed her own raven black hair beautifully. She sighed inwardly that her own brown and gold outfit could never give her the air of sophistication that Sheila created, not when her button nose practically got lost between her brown eyes.

'There are the Grand Teton Mountains.' Logan's voice was quiet as his arm swept out before him.

She had never ceased being conscious of the mountains spreading before her, but now Jennifer stopped beside him to stare in awe at the magnificent citadels.

'The tall, jagged peak towering over the rest is Grand Teton himself, 13,770 feet above sea level. There to the north, the flat-topped one is Mount Moran. Below us is the Snake River. It looks peaceful now, but those ripples hide its muscles. The Snake is born here in the Teton Wilderness Area. It twists and turns its way through Yellowstone Park and back through the Grand Tetons before gathering the strength to rage through Hell's Canyon in Idaho where it's earned the name "The River of No Return".' Her eyes followed his pointing hand eagerly, filled with a longing to be a part of this unearthly splendour. 'Are you impressed with the United States version of Switzerland, Jenny? I don't believe there's any place on this earth that can surpass the Grand Tetons and the Wind River Range in this kind of rugged, untouched beauty. It may be equalled but never surpassed.'

She nodded her head in a breathless agreement, casting a shy glance up at Logan to see his intense interest in her reaction. His mouth lifted quickly into that familiar smile.

'Did you know we have a lake named after you here in the Park?' he teased.

'After me?'

'Jenny Lake. Actually it was named for a Shoshone Indian woman.'

'Tell me about it,' she urged.

'She was the wife of one of the more colourful characters in the Grand Tetons' history, Richard

137

Leigh, more commonly known as Beaver Dick. He was born in England, though he fought in the U.S./ Mexican War of the 1840s. He came to the Rocky Mountains to live, and later he guided a government geological survey team through the Snake River Canyon. As a result a lake was named after him, Leigh Lake, and one for his wife, Jenny.'

'And?' She sensed there was more to the story. 'What about his wife Jenny?'

'The entire family was snowbound one winter in a one-room cabin. They all contracted smallpox. Jenny was the first to die. With no knowledge and virtually no medicine and Leigh sick himself, he struggled to save them, but within four days he had lost his wife and all six children. He remarried later and had another family, but years later, he admitted that visiting a place filled with memories of Jenny and their children brought tears to his eyes.'

The long-ago tragedy silenced Jennifer as she gazed back at the mountain range, never changing, never revealing any hint of the many things they had seen.

'Want some cocoa?' Logan offered, opening the thermos jug that had been tucked under one arm.

Jennifer nodded, then glanced around to see where Dirk and Sheila were. They were standing some distance away, with Dirk gesturing with his hands towards a specific mountain. Logan's eyes followed Jennifer's. Her face paled when she finally looked back at him, though his expression revealed nothing of the inner jealousy she knew he must feel at the attentive expression on Sheila's face.

'I suppose they're discussing exactly what colour the pines are in this light,' said Logan, his eyes again on Jennifer.

'I suppose,' she agreed, watching him pour the steaming cocoa into a cup and hand it to her.

'Have you decided what you're going to do yet?'

An underlying tone of sharpness edged his voice in the casual question. Jennifer's hand trembled for a brief minute.

'You mean about Minneapolis?' She knew very well what he meant, but she wanted time to think about her answer.

'And your Mr. Stevenson.'

'He's hardly "my" Mr. Stevenson.' Her laugh was too nervous to sound genuine.

'I got a different impression. But you certainly are taking a long time making up your mind whether or not to accept his marriage proposal.'

'I don't think marriage was part of what he proposed,' Jennifer shrugged, a cynical twist in the smile on her lips.

Logan had been staring at mountains as if the idle conversation meant nothing to him, but at her wry statement, he turned his penetrating gaze on her.

'A little affair, huh?' sarcastically. 'And you're holding out for a ring.'

'Perhaps.' Her eyes strayed to the distant pair so engrossed in their conversation that they were unaware of anyone else. 'Perhaps I'm just waiting to see my sister settled, before. . . .' Her voice trailed into silence.

'Do you mean that when Sheila gets married you're

actually considering going back to that man?' There was no masking the anger in Logan's face or voice as he stepped almost threateningly towards her.

She couldn't help noticing, with sinking heart, he said 'when Sheila marries', not 'if'.

'Don't point fingers, Logan,' she jeered, raising her head defiantly. 'You're far from immune to strange pretty skirts. I believe I stand as proof to that! I recall that not ten minutes after kissing my sister under the mistletoe you were trying to inflict yourself on me!'

'I could shake you until your teeth rattled!'

Her cup of cocoa was jarred to the ground as he imprisoned her shoulders in a vicious grip. She stifled a cry of pain as he jerked her to his chest where her frightened eyes stared into his blazingly angry ones. His gaze left hers to travel over her flushed cheeks, to stop on her parted lips. Her heart hammered wildly against her ribs.

'I think I've proved my point,' she managed to speak, although her voice was shaky.

His eyes returned to meet hers, bemused, the anger gone.

'I think I've learned something, too, Jenny Glenn. You're not totally immune to me either.'

'Let me go!' she whispered angrily, averting her eyes before he could see more there than she wanted him to. 'I don't want you to touch me!'

'Don't you?' he smiled.

'No! You're a despicable, arrogant playboy and I hate you! You could never be faithful to anything but your own lustful desires.' Her fear of her own emotions brought her close to tears. 'When I think of how Sheila dotes on every word you say. . . .'

'You don't know me very well, nor your sister either.' Logan's eyes were mocking as he set her away from him. 'But I believe you'll change your mind, in time.'

'That's what you think!' She tried to put as much scorn and haughty disregard as she could into her voice. But she only succeeded in feeling childish as Logan's lilting chuckle battered her words. 'I'll . . . I'll never bow to you the way Sheila does.'

No, somehow, she thought to herself, her pride would prevent her love from showing and deflect the telling blow of humilation and embarrassment.

A spark of rekindled anger flared briefly in Logan's brown eyes before it was replaced with amusement.

'Some day you'll regret that vitriolic tongue of yours when you try my temper too far. But in the end, Jenny Glenn, you'll yield. . . .' He broke off his sentence and smiled over Jennifer's shoulder at the approaching couple. 'Ready for some sandwiches and cocoa?'

'Good idea,' Dirk smiled, his eyes resting intimately on Sheila, who quickly cast her own gaze down while murmuring agreement.

They all tramped through the snow and across the road to the jeep together. Somehow, Jennifer was never quite sure how he arranged it, Logan settled himself in the back seat with her, opening the picnic hamper and passing the sandwiches, then packing the remnants back in when all their appetites had been satisfied. With galling nonchalance he tossed the ignition keys to Dirk, suggesting he drive the rest of the way.

Despite the breathtaking scenery that was shown to her for the balance of the afternoon, Jennifer was miserable. Logan's intimate glances, the touch of his hand on her arm when he wanted to draw her attention somewhere else, all served to increase her already jittery nerves. She knew he was just using her to take his attention off Sheila and Dirk in the front seat, but she couldn't match his casual, flirtatious manner. There was nothing frivolous about her love for him and her emotions were too serious to indulge lightly in his meaningless attention.

When Dirk, at last, parked in front of Sheila's house, it was all Jennifer could do to keep from bolting out of the jeep. She managed to wait politely for Logan to open her door and express her gratitude for the trip. But she could tell by the gleam of amusement in his eyes that he knew she could hardly wait to get into the house. She finally managed to stammer a good-bye to Dirk and flee inside, away from Logan's mocking eyes.

# CHAPTER NINE

'GOOD morning, Jenny!' Sheila sang out gaily, the long blue and lavender print housecoat giving the effect that she was floating into the kitchen instead of walking.

'Good morning,' Jenny replied, sighing as she glanced down at her own robe, a washed-out apple green sateen that stopped short of her knees. It could only be classified as adolescent, she decided. There was no chance of it matching the elegance of Sheila's.

'I have a feeling it's going to be a spectacularly gorgeous day!' her sister exclaimed. The radiant expression on her face seemed to have attained an even greater glow than had been present in the past week.

'Do you realize how long it's been since I've been skiing? I think I made it once last year.' Sheila poured herself a cup of coffee before sitting at the table with Jennifer. 'You're really going to enjoy it, Jenny.'

'Will you *please* stop calling me Jenny! My name is Jennifer!'

'I ... I didn't realize you were so touchy about it any more,' Sheila apologized, momentarily taken aback by her sister's unexpected display of temper.

'I'm not really,' Jennifer was immediately contrite. 'I got up on the wrong side of the bed this morning, I guess.'

'This hasn't been the only morning. Honey, what's been bothering you lately? You just haven't been yourself, not since that Brad fellow left, but even more so this past week. You always seem to be going off by yourself. Can't you tell me about it?' cajoled Sheila. 'I heard you tossing and turning all night last night and there's circles under your eyes this morning. We've always been able to talk before, though I'll admit I've been almost too busy since you've been here to really sit down and hash anything over. But today—well, I've got the whole day, or at least, most of it.'

'Sheila, you are the dearest sister in the whole world,' Jennifer reached out and squeezed her sister's hand affectionately, 'and I wouldn't trade you for a dozen of anyone else. It's just that I have some problems that I've got to work out for myself.'

'That's what I'm getting at. Talk them over with me. Between the two of us, we could work out whatever's bothering you.'

'No, you can't.' Jennifer shook her head sadly.

'Is it Brad?'

'Partly.' She ran a hand through her hair, wispy strands reflecting red in the morning sunlight. 'You might as well know I've been considering going back to Minneapolis.'

'Jenny ... Jennifer,' Sheila corrected herself. 'You're not going back to work for him?'

'No.'

'Then why go? I know lately you've been unhappy, but at first you really seemed to be enjoying yourself

144

here. I know the children just love having you. They'd be positively lost without you.'

'Not for long. It's just that I feel so useless.' Jennifer held up a hand to stave off the protest that Sheila was about to utter. 'I know I've pulled my share of the load and really lifted some of the burdens off your shoulders for a while, but I spent quite a bit of time and money on my secretarial schooling. Besides, I think I would be making a pretty good guess if I said that quite soon there's going to be someone else who's going to look after you and the children permanently.' Sheila blushed beautifully as Jennifer's morale slipped a notch lower. 'And I'm just not any good playing the mouse in the corner.' She tried to laugh.

'If it's a job that's worrying you, I'm sure Logan could arrange....'

'No!' Jennifer interrupted sharply before tempering her voice. 'I'm capable of getting a job for myself. I just really think I should go back to Minneapolis. It was silly for me to run away from there in the first place.' It had turned out to be the biggest mistake of her life.

'When were you planning on leaving?'

'I hadn't got that far.' Her mind cried soon, very soon.

'Well, I hope you stay for a while longer, for personal reasons,' Sheila beamed, her brilliant blue eyes revealing her secret happiness.

Jennifer couldn't give an honest reply to that statement, so she made none at all.

'I have a few errands to do in town. Is there anything you need while I'm there?' Jennifer offered instead.

'No, I don't think so. Don't forget we're going skiing this afternoon.'

'I won't,' Jennifer retorted quickly, walking out of the kitchen towards the bedrooms to dress.

'I mean it.' Sheila followed behind her. 'No excuses and no cakes in the oven or any of those other tricks you've used this last week whenever Logan has made plans for something.'

'And we mustn't upset Logan's plans.' A teasing smile hid the caustic sarcasm in Jennifer's voice.

'Honestly, Jenny, he planned it specially for you, so the least you can do is come. I want your promise you'll be there.'

'I'll be there,' Jennifer assured her emphatically before disappearing inside her bedroom.

Minutes later, dressed in her russet brown and gold ski outfit, Jennifer hurried out the door with Sheila's voice ringing after her, reminding her to be at the slopes by one o'clock.

She shuffled dejectedly through the snow once out of sight of the house. It had been unbearable this last week with Logan constantly forcing her to be the fourth. At first, it wasn't so bad. Jennifer had almost thought that Dirk had a chance at winning, but it only took one look at Sheila's face when she exchanged glances with Logan to understand the secret intimacy between them. And last night—last night had been the crushing blow.

The children had been in bed. Jennifer had

146

attempted to sink into the forgetfulness of sleep, but it had been denied her. Instead she had sat alone in the darkened living room trying to fight off the depression that hung over her head like thunder clouds on the Teton peaks. Then she had heard the crunching sound of snow as a car halted in front of the house. Although tempted to peep out the window, she had resisted, suffering her imagination rather than see what was really happening. Finally the sound of car doors opening and closing followed by Sheila's laughter, had roused her from the chair.

She would never forget the horrible pain that gripped her when she had seen Sheila step into Logan's arms and plant a kiss on his lips before he lovingly walked her to the door, an arm firmly wrapped around her shoulders hugging her to his side. Jennifer had run swiftly into her bedroom feigning sleep when Sheila had later glanced in. And this morning, Sheila had practically come right out and said that she and Logan were getting married.

Jennifer sighed deeply as she stepped off the kerb into the street. Simultaneously a horn blared loudly in her ear and a hand jerked her quickly backwards as a car drove past just inches from her.

'You'd better watch where you're going,' a middle-aged man reprimanded her. 'You very nearly got yourself killed!'

'Th-thank you,' Jennifer stammered. 'I'm afraid I was daydreaming.'

'Daydreaming and walking in traffic don't mix.'

'They certainly don't,' she agreed shakily. 'Thank

you again.'

The man tipped his stetson cowboy hat and walked on. This time Jennifer looked carefully before crossing the street. For a brief moment she wondered how much easier it would have been if the car had hit her, before shaking the morbid thought off. That was wishing an accident on herself, she thought with a shudder, a coward's form of suicide.

Reaching the shopping centre, Jennifer idly glanced in the shop windows as she strolled by. The only reason she had come to town was to get away. Oh, she could stop to see if her watch was repaired, maybe splurge on some perfume or cosmetics, but it was mostly a form of escape. Too bad she couldn't escape this afternoon's skiing outing, she grimaced. She increased her pace as she recognized the jeweller's sign just ahead of her.

As she drew even with the display window, Jennifer glanced inside. With a tightening throat she saw Logan standing inside, a clerk hovering beside him with a small black velvet ring box in his hand. Logan was smiling in approval, taking the box out of the clerk's hands and placing it in his pocket. When he turned towards the door, Jennifer ducked quickly into an adjoining store, the pain constricting her chest until she could hardly breathe.

'An engagement ring!' her heart cried. 'For Sheila!'

Blindly she watched him stride by, lithe and handsome. She hurried out of the store and into the jeweller's, hesitating, like a deer about to flee from danger, just inside the door. The clerk that had been with Logan was talking to another younger clerk.

'Diamonds always seemed so much more acceptable as engagement rings to me,' the younger one was saying.

'You certainly can't accuse Logan of settling for something cheaper. That stone must have cost him a fortune and with that circlet of diamonds around it—well! He told me it was a tradition in the Taylor family that all prospective brides receive an engagement ring of——'

Jennifer involuntarily emitted a cry at his words, causing the older clerk to cut off his sentence and turn to her solicitously.

'Can I help you, miss?' he inquired.

'No, no, thank you.' And she dashed out of the door.

As Jennifer approached the chair lift, she didn't need a second glance to recognize the figure striding towards her in a bright blue and black jacket and black ski pants. His yellow snow goggles were pushed back from his face, offering her no protection from his angry eyes.

'Do you realize it's half past one?' Logan questioned sharply.

'My watch is being repaired. I didn't realize it was so late.' Her own dark-tinted goggles were in place, hiding her pained expression from his penetrating eyes.

'There are a lot of things you haven't realized lately.' He gripped her arm firmly, pushing her ahead of him, two pair of skis firmly clamped under his other arm. 'I told Sheila not to let you out of her sight today, to lead

149

you here if necessary.'

'I promised her I would come. She knew I'd keep my word.'

'The way you've been dodging things this past week, I wouldn't have been at all surprised if you hadn't shown up today.' He glared at her as they stopped, and dropped the skis on the ground in front of her. 'I was just getting ready to look for you, to drag you here by force if I had to.'

'And now you're angry because I came and you didn't get that thrill of knowing you were solely responsible for having everything just the way you wanted it,' she lashed out bitterly, wishing her sharp words would cut as deep as his.

'I don't know what's eating you.' Anger was etched in the line of his jaw and the grim set of his mouth. 'But yes, today is important to me, and I would like everything to be just right. I once thought Sheila's happiness was important to you, too, but I guess that's changed, hasn't it?'

Even though masked by her dark glasses, Jennifer couldn't meet his gaze. She did want Sheila to be happy, but she couldn't help wishing that her sister's happiness was not found in the arms of the man she loved. Ever since leaving the jewellers', she had been telling herself that she was fortunate to find out for sure that Logan and Sheila were going to be married, that now she had an opportunity to adjust to it privately and manage to put on a convincing show when it was actually presented to her as an accomplished fact. But it wasn't as easy as that. Just seeing Logan brought the aching torment to the surface.

Logan was bending near her feet, shoving her boots into the skis as if they were inanimate objects not attached to her body. His roughness forced her to grab his shoulder to keep from being thrown off balance into the snow. His muscles tightened at her touch. Quickly she released her hold as if she had touched a high-voltage wire and was recoiling from the shock.

'Where's Sheila?' Jennifer asked hurriedly as Logan bent to buckle his own skis.

'I sent them on up to the top,' pausing sarcastically, 'when I thought I'd have to go looking for you.'

So the foursome was complete once more, Jennifer thought bitterly. And poor Dirk was to be included as a witness to Logan's victory, too.

She avoided Logan's guiding hand as they joined the line waiting for the chair-lift. Minutes later they were aboard the lift and swinging towards the top. She glanced bleakly at Logan out of the corner of her eye, the dark gold stocking cap that had been in his pocket completely covered his chestnut brown hair and the yellow-tinted goggles made his brown eyes look amber. But there was no relief in the arrogant flare of his nose, or the grim line of his mouth. Nor was there any relief for the dull ache throbbing in Jennifer's heart.

Then they were at the top, swinging off the chairs on to their skis, gliding silently across the snow, the chattering, laughing voices of other skiers mocking their sober, quiet faces. They stopped at the edge of the first slope. Jennifer planted her poles in the snow while she adjusted her hat and mittens. She could hardly bear the gnawing tension that grew with each progressive minute of silence.

'Sheila told me you've decided to go back to Minneapolis.' Harshness seeped through his calm statement.

'That's right.' Jennifer's chin lifted mutinously.

'You're going to accept that man's—what should I call it?—proposition.' His degrading words cut through her like a sword.

The wind whistled out of the grey leaden clouds above them, picking up the snow at their feet and sending it dancing down the slope.

'Would it do any good to ask you to stay longer?' Logan sighed in exasperated anger. 'For Sheila's sake. if nothing else?'

Jennifer's mouth twisted bitterly. How typically presumptuous of him to think that all he had to do was ask.

'Jenny——' he began. His voice possessed a commandingly tender tone that wrenched at her self-control.

'Don't call me that!' she cried huskily, with tears brimming her eyes.

Grabbing her ski poles, she flipped herself expertly around so that she was facing down the slope. Before Logan's outstretched hand could stop her, she was pushing off to race down the ski run.

In seconds she was careering down the hill, the trees blurring into a solid wall on either side and the other skiers were faceless objects to be zigzagged around. 'Too fast! You're going too fast!' The alarm bell rang in her head. The sound of another pair of skis slushing after her urged her to strain for every ounce of speed she could muster.

'Slow down!' Logan ordered as he drew alongside.

For one brief instant, she toyed with the idea of maintaining her breakneck speed. A broken leg, a broken neck, weren't they better than a broken heart? Then she straightened, making her sweeps wider down the run until she turned her skis at right angles and braked to a halt.

'What were you trying to do, kill yourself?' Logan's rage unleashed itself as he stopped in front of her, blocking her way down the mountain.

Her face was drained of all colour while her knees trembled weakly beneath her. The cold air burned her lungs as she gasped for breath.

'You're not going to answer me, as usual,' he muttered angrily as Jennifer continued to avoid his face. 'If you're not lashing out at me with that damned barbed tongue of yours, then you're running away. When are you going to stop fighting me and——'

'Oh, look, there's Sheila and Dirk!' Jennifer exclaimed breathlessly, recognizing the bright blue ski suit with the moulding white stripe down the side that belonged to Sheila.

She waved frantically at them, glad of anything that would offer her a respite of Logan's presence. At last Sheila spotted them and waved back gaily. Jennifer could sense that Logan gave in with fuming reluctance. His only comment was a biting order to keep their pace down. As Logan and Jennifer neared the other couple, Sheila and Dirk set out down the hill, with Sheila darting back and forth in front of the more staid and cautious Dirk.

In the blink of an eye, the scene changed. There was a spray of snow, a sharp ringing cry, and a cartwheeling blue and white figure erupting in front of Jennifer. Then, almost in slow motion, she saw Dirk's red jacket rushing to the prone woman in blue at the same time that Logan left her side and hurled himself towards both of them.

'Sheila!' A sobbing sound was involuntarily drawn from Jennifer's lips.

By the time she reached the group, a member of the ski patrol had already joined with Logan in examining her sister for any broken bones while Dirk painstakingly brushed the snow from her face. Jennifer stood silently to one side, watching Logan carefully removing Sheila's skis. Her sister's eyes fluttered open and she moaned softly.

'It looks as if it's just the right foot,' Logan told the man from the ski patrol.

'Right. I'll go and get the basket sled and alert them below to contact an ambulance,' he replied before skiing away.

Jennifer felt so apart from the scene, as if she was looking into someone else's nightmare. Her anxious eyes were fixed on Logan's tight-lipped face as he spoke with Dirk. She didn't hear what was said, only felt the cold chilling shock at her sister's inert body. Time became an immeasurable thing. It seemed so long before the ski patrol returned, wrapped her sister in blankets, and tied her into the basket sled, but it probably had only been a matter of minutes. Although they were halfway down the mountainside already, their skis made such slow progress to the bottom. She was half conscious of Logan by her side, but her attention was focused on Sheila.

At the hospital Jennifer had still not shaken off that peculiar dazed feeling. There was Dirk pacing the waiting room floor. Logan was somewhere in one of the admitting offices filling out those long, interminable forms. And she was sitting on the green tweed couch, the cup of coffee still clutched tightly in her hands. Logan had given it to her shortly after they had wheeled Sheila in, ordered her to take a drink, waited long enough to see that she did, and then he had left. The rest of the coffee had long been cold. A hand touched her shoulder and she jumped.

'You never drank the coffee,' Logan said softly, removing the cup from her hands and placing it on the table. 'Are you all right?'

Jennifer shook her head numbly.

'Sheila?' she asked.

'They've taken her up to X-ray. She should be down shortly,' Logan told her, his eyes following Dirk's nervous pacing. 'She put a ski pole through her foot. The doctor thinks she's probably broken a bone as well.'

A man of medium height dressed in the pale green hospital uniform walked into the room. A woman in white appeared at his side, glancing at the group in the waiting room before she spoke. Jennifer caught the

155

muffled words 'sister' and 'fiancé' as the man nodded his head and turned to walk towards them.

'It's good to see you, Logan.' The man reached out and shook Logan's hand affably. 'I would prefer it under different circumstances, as I'm sure you would. You must be Miss Glenn.' He turned to Jennifer, then to the impatient Dirk. 'Mr Hamilton. I'm Doctor March.'

Jennifer tried to concentrate on his words when he began to explain Sheila's condition. But the only words that penetrated were 'puncture' and 'a fracture of the tarsal bone in her foot'.

'I have her under mild sedation now. If you'd like to see her for a few minutes, you may,' he finished calmly.

Jennifer clutched Logan's hand tightly as he helped her from the couch and led her down a hallway to Sheila. She stared down at her sister silently, hardly recognizing the pale face surrounded by a cloud of black hair. Then her eyelids fluttered open, revealing the brilliant blue eyes that were her sister's trademark. Jennifer smiled down at this fragile china doll who had always before seemed so indestructible.

'Hello,' Sheila said thickly. 'I really did it good this time, huh?'

'You certainly did,' Logan smiled, filling in the silence when Jennifer had only been able to nod. 'We can't stay. Dirk's outside waiting to see you.'

'The children?' Sheila raised her head weakly from her pillow.

'We'll take care of them, don't worry,' Logan assured

156

her. 'We'll come back to see you later when you're not so groggy.'

Logan had already guided her to the doorway when Jennifer finally found her voice and managed a tremulous good-bye to her sister. He led her back into the waiting room, set her on the couch and told her to wait for him

While Logan had gone, Jennifer fought to get a grip on herself. She knew the strain of this last month had weakened her, but now Sheila needed her more than ever, especially the children. She had to get control of her nerves before she saw Eric and Cindy. They were so dependent on their mother, their only parent left, that she just had to make sure that they didn't become over-emotional as she had done.

If only she could appear as calm as Logan, she thought, watching him come confidently towards her. She managed a brief but composed smile as she met his questioning glance.

'Ready to go?' he asked.

Jennifer nodded. Once outside the hospital, Logan reached over and removed the russet brown cap from her head. The sudden coolness of the brisk afternoon air was a refreshing balm to her tense nerves.

'What did you do that for?' Jennifer asked, automatically shaking her head, enjoying the feel of the cool wind playing through her red-gold hair.

'So you could shake away some of that fear and tension that's built up inside you,' Logan smiled. Instantly Jennifer was captured by the comforting warmth of his gaze.

*Sheila.* She must remember Sheila and not let her personal feelings interfere. Not now, later when she was alone, but not now, she ordered herself.

Although the ride to Sheila's house was made in silence, it wasn't the same as the cocoon of silence that had surrounded Jennifer after the accident. This was companionable, and she drew strength from it. When Logan slowed the car to a stop, Jennifer turned and began to offer her thanks.

'Would you like me to come with you while you tell the children?' Logan interrupted before she could finish.

'Would you?' Her smile was shaky with relief at his offer. For all her hard-won composure, Jennifer didn't really want to face Eric and Cindy alone.

'Of course. I planned to all along.' His teasing smile did flip-flops to her heart as he opened the car door and stepped outside. She followed suit.

They had barely entered the front door when they were accosted by two accusing children.

'Where have you been?' Cindy asked in false anger.

'Where's Mom?' Eric's voice expressed the alarm that Cindy had tried to hide.

As calmly and as patiently as she could, Jennifer explained what had happened. She understood the panic-stricken looks. Mothers were supposed to be invulnerable to those kind of things. But somehow, with Logan's steadying presence, they managed to accept it and—Jennifer said a silent prayer of gratitude—even to see a bit of humour in it, thanks to Logan. He had stepped in and made it an adventure to them. Before

Jennifer knew what was happening, they had talked Logan into staying for supper, instinctively seizing on his idea and using it to ensure his acceptance of their invitation.

A smile of pleasure played on Jennifer's lips as she realized that it hadn't taken much coaxing on their part to get him to agree. Of course, it was for the children's sake, she reminded herself. But still, it didn't hurt too much to indulge in a little wishful thinking. When she glanced at the clock, Jennifer was surprised to see how late it was. The question of supper was not premature. She excused herself quickly and hurried into the kitchen, knowing this was going to be a special meal and not just to boost the children's spirits either.

When Jennifer called them in to supper, it was with a certain pride, knowing that the meal of pork chops, steamed rice with tomato gravy, crisp celery stalks stuffed with cheese, and pineapple upside-down cake for dessert, though it was a simple meal, was attractive to the eye as well as deliciously edible.

There was so much laughter and chatter at the table that evening, Jennifer found it difficult to remember that Sheila was lying in a hospital bed. Only when her sister's eyes laughed at her from Eric's face was the realization brought back with a slightly sobering effect. But she didn't let it tarnish her evening. To Jennifer, seated across the table from Logan, watching his smiling face as he listened interestedly to a long dissertation by Eric on the things that were wrong with school, this was a stolen hour, one she could cherish and dream about, she and Logan seated at a table, a brown-eyed pair of children on either side with winking dimples on each cheek.

His eyes locked with hers with such an intense intimacy in his gaze that she felt he had slipped into her thoughts and seen what her imagination had conjured up. She managed to break the spell and hide the rosy blush that had begun to steal into her face, with a flurry of activity, gathering plates and passing out the dessert.

'I forgot to tell you, Jenny,' Logan said with a mock seriousness. 'We got roped into a game of Chinese Checkers.'

'Girlth againth the boyth,' Cindy inserted quickly.

'How did "we" manage to do that?' Jennifer laughed.

'It was easy,' said Eric. 'I dared him.'

'And I double-dared him,' Cindy joined in.

'So you see.' Logan tilted his head in resignation. 'What could I do?'

'Exactly!' Eric agreed enthusiastically.

'Hmm. What would happen if I double-dared all of you to do the dishes?' Jennifer glanced around the table at the horrified looks of astonishment on Eric's and Cindy's faces.

'It doesn't work for that,' Eric gulped.

'I think it works for stacking dishes,' Logan stated. 'Otherwise Jenny might not think that double-dare was any good for Chinese Checkers.'

With a speed previously unheard-of when it came to household chores, the two children had the dishes scraped and stacked and the game spread out on the kitchen table.

After two games, with each side winning one, Jennifer looked up to the kitchen clock and announced that it was bedtime. The grumblings and pleadings were swept aside when Logan announced that if they were ready for bed in ten minutes, he'd read them a story.

Standing over the kitchen sink, her hands immersed in dishwater, Jennifer listened to the rhythmic sound of Logan's voice as he read to the two children in the other room. As she placed the last pan on the draining-board, an overwhelming tiredness engulfed her. The utter futility of trying to believe that this evening could ever be repeated in the future drained what happiness she had felt. The almost sinful guilt of wanting what belonged to her sister rested heavily on her shoulders. She should be the one lying in that hospital bed, not Sheila. If only the accident had happened to her! Two lonely, solitary tears rolled slowly down her cheeks.

'It's been a long day for you, hasn't it, Jenny Glenn?' Logan stood by the counter staring down at her, his gaze so tender and compassionate that the two tears Jennifer had wiped so quickly away at the sound of his voice were replaced by two more.

If he hadn't spoken her name in that gentle caressing tone, she might have been able to resist him when he drew her into his arms. Instead Jennifer went meekly, his arms firmly encircling her, holding her close against his chest. Although she wanted to cry buckets of tears, the ache was too deep and painful. She stilled the wild singing of her heart, forbidding it to become enamoured by the possessive touch of his hand on her head

161

or the rock-hardness of his muscles. But in her imagination she felt the erratic pulse of his heart matching hers. Then a familiar shape made itself felt to her hand as it rested on his chest. The jutting square burned her fingers as she slowly disengaged herself from his embrace. She shivered momentarily, not just because she had left the warmth of his arms, but because of the engagement ring still in his pocket.

'You'll want to see Sheila yet tonight,' wishing the huskiness didn't betray her jumbled emotions so blatantly.

'It's already after visiting hours, but I'm sure I'll be able to stop in for a few minutes,' Logan agreed, studying her intently as he spoke.

'I shouldn't have let the children talk you into staying.'

'They didn't,' Logan corrected her. He stepped towards her, but halted when Jennifer moved involuntarily away. 'You need a good night's rest.'

'Thanks for telling me how great I look,' Jennifer thought bitterly before chiding herself for the unwarranted criticism.

'I'll pick you up in the morning around nine-thirty. We can be at the hospital when the doctor makes his rounds.'

Jennifer nodded that she would be ready.

'You will call me tonight, if you need anything?' His question was sharp and rebuking. 'I'll be staying at my mother's. Her number is listed there by the phone.'

She agreed, assuring him politely that there would be no need for her to call, that everything was fine.

Logan left, almost reluctantly, Jennifer thought, then laughed at the idea. He probably could hardly wait to get to the hospital.

Dressing for bed, Jennifer thought sleep would surely be denied her, but the tension, anxiety, and strain of the day had tired her more than she realized. Within minutes after her head touched the pillow, she was asleep.

# CHAPTER TEN

MRS. TAYLOR, Logan's mother, was in the waiting room when Logan and Jennifer left Sheila the next morning. Her sister had been in very gay spirits, laughing at her accident and generally impressing the doctor with assurances that she was very much better. There had been no ring on her finger which made Jennifer decide that Logan wanted to wait until she was out of hospital, and the ring could be given with a bit more ceremony. She was glad she hadn't to carry on much conversation with her sister, except to answer questions about the children. Jennifer hated the jealousy that had consumed her each time she watched Logan and Sheila together. Her surprise at seeing Logan's mother was quickly hidden. After all, Sheila was her future daughter-in-law.

'I have something I want to talk over with you, Jenny,' said Logan, ushering her over to a chair next to his mother. 'I discussed it with Mother last night, and she's in favour of it, so I brought her along for moral support.'

Jennifer frowned, 'What is it?'

Logan took a deep breath, glanced almost apprehensively at his mother before he began.

'Doctor March said that he would be releasing

164

Sheila tomorrow. She'll probably be in considerable pain the first few days which, whether she would admit it or not, would make her a little short-tempered with the children.' Logan paused, examining Jennifer's face for her reaction. 'I suggested that Cindy and Eric stay with the Jeffries for a week.'

'I think that's a good idea.' Jennifer was puzzled by his attempt to handle such a suggestion so delicately.

'That's not all. I have to go back to the ranch. There are some things there I have to attend to personally. Knowing Sheila as I do, I know she's going to be concerned about the Lodge, because it's for sure she won't be able to work for at least a week. If she stays here in town, the temptation is going to be too great to keep her from going down there. I want her to convalesce at the ranch for a week.'

'I see.' Jennifer hesitated. She could tell there was more to it than that. 'I don't know why she wouldn't agree. I could work down at the Lodge in her place.'

'No.' His mouth tightened at her suggestion. 'Mother can take care of the Lodge. She ran it for a good many years, and she'd enjoy taking over the reins for a week. No, you'll come to the ranch with Sheila.'

'What!' Jennifer stared first at Logan, then at his mother. He couldn't possibly mean it!

'It's the only thing to do, dear,' Mrs. Taylor spoke up. 'It just wouldn't be right for your sister to spend a week there, all alone with Logan. But if you were there—well, the two of you together would sort of chaperone each other.'

'That's impossible!' Jennifer cried, jumping out of

165

her chair, her hands twisting together nervously. 'Sheila can stay at the house. I can look after her there and make sure she doesn't go wandering off to the Lodge.'

'It wouldn't work,' Logan said sharply. 'You know how headstrong she is. She'd have you talked into taking her there for therapy before two days had gone by. No, the solution is the ranch.'

'I won't go!' Jennifer declared, her eyes blazing defiantly into his.

'You will!' Logan reached out and captured her wrist in a fierce and bruising grip. There was a savage ruthlessness in his expression as he twisted her closer to him. 'You will go because she's your sister, and right now she needs you, a member of her own family. Go home, pack clothes for both of you, and I'll pick you up tomorrow morning at eleven o'clock sharp. And so help me, Jenny, you'd better be there waiting for me!'

With that, her wrist was released and Logan walked arrogantly away. When Jennifer turned towards Mrs. Taylor, she knew her breathing was ragged and her face flushed.

'I must apologize for my son,' Mrs. Taylor said softly, an indulgent smile on her face. 'I'm sure he didn't mean to get so sharp with you. I'm afraid he takes after his father a bit when it comes to that temper of his. Once my Rob decided on something, he'd fly into a rage if his plans were thwarted.'

'I don't understand why it's so important....' Jennifer stopped before the sobbing in her heart moved to her voice.

'Jenny——' Mrs. Taylor hesitated. 'Our ranch is

166

very beautiful and peaceful. It would be the perfect place for Sheila to rest and relax. I can't help but feel you would like our home very much.'

'I'm sure I would,' Jennifer agreed, adding silently to herself that anywhere Logan was would be beautiful.

'Won't you please agree to go with your sister? I'm sure she wouldn't understand your reluctance to go with her.'

Jennifer's eyes flashed sharply at Amanda Taylor, sensing there was more meaning in her cryptic statement, that perhaps she had guessed Jennifer's true feelings towards Logan. But the twinkling brown eyes smiled innocently back at her.

'You can tell Logan I'll be ready at eleven. Now, if you'll excuse me, I have a lot to do between now and then.' She realized her voice was bitter and just slightly sarcastic, but Jennifer had lost another battle with Logan Taylor. Now she needed to re-group in private so that she could face the week ahead with some degree of dignity in order to prevent the final humiliation of Logan discovering her love for him.

Jennifer added another log to the fire already blazing cheerfully away in the fireplace. Mrs. Taylor had been right; she had fallen in love with the ranch at first sight. It was nestled snugly on the lee side of a mountain, a sturdy row of pines sheltering the buildings from the winter winds. The rustic barns, stables, and outbuildings were surrounded by a picturesque buckrail fence. But it was the house that had called to her, saying,

'This is home.' It wasn't rambling and grand, or white and elegant. Its two-storey roof was steep to shed the heavy snows, and there was a wide screened porch on the side to watch the evening sunset. The walls were stained native wood, strong and thick and promising shelter from the cold winds. Perhaps it was the way the sun had reflected off the windows that had given Jennifer such an overwhelming feeling of being welcomed home.

Logan had explained, once he had brought them inside the house, that the upstairs was now closed off in the winters, as well as the dining room and parlour. A simple matter of heat conservation, he had said, in spite of the installation of central heating. But Jennifer hadn't minded, not when she had the cosy panelled living room with the large stone fireplace to sit in front of all day. The meals were taken in the kitchen, except for Sheila who was restricted to the large master bedroom the first two days. Logan had seen to it there was a day bed in the bedroom so that Sheila wouldn't have to take the risk of having her foot bumped sharing the big double bed with Jennifer. Logan slept in the little room off the kitchen that had been used by the housekeeper in former days.

All in all, it hadn't been as difficult as Jennifer had imagined it would be. Logan was gone from dawn to dusk. The first morning the sound of dishes in the kitchen had wakened her and the later slamming of the door had confirmed that he was up and gone. The evenings he spent in the house, sharing a meal with Jennifer across the kitchen table. That could have been

168

so intimate except for his indifference. No, it wasn't really indifference so much as lack of interest. And that, Jennifer found, was something she could bear. After dinner, Logan went in to see Sheila while Jennifer occupied herself with dishes and later television. They could have been two strangers merely sharing the same roof.

But Jennifer had found a way to dull the pain of being so near to him, yet so far away. She could take care of his home, cook his meals, including breakfast, and do all the little things that a wife would do. There had been times, especially when Logan was with Sheila, that the old jealousy and longing would steal back on her, but she managed to remain composed when his brown eyes met hers, or even gay and happy when she was with Sheila. She really felt she deserved an award for hiding her torment so well.

The big Black Forest cuckoo clock called out to her twice and she straightened up from her kneeling place by the fire, smoothing her blue jeans as she rose. Through the open doorway to the bedroom, Jennifer could hear her sister's voice, evidently still on the telephone with Dirk, who had called at least twice a day since they had arrived. Sheila hadn't seemed to object either, accepting the calls with a calmness that surprised Jennifer.

She sighed heavily before making her way into the kitchen. Baking a cake for dessert that night would at least take her mind away from her unhappy thoughts. The sound of footsteps in the snow followed by the banging of the back door halted her. Logan was standing outside, a large black object cradled in his arms.

'Get me some of those big terry towels out of the linen closet,' he said briskly as she opened the door and let him in.

One look at the lifeless baby calf sent Jennifer scurrying to carry out his order. He had taken the calf in by the fireplace when she returned. Taking one of the towels from her hand, he began rubbing the black body roughly.

'What happened?' Jennifer asked as she knelt down beside him.

'He was born out of season. His mother just abandoned him,' Logan replied. 'Warm some milk up for him. There's some bottles in the lower right-hand cupboard by the sink you can put it in.'

In minutes she had the milk scalded, poured in the bottle, found the black nursing nipple in one of the drawers and was back in the living room. At the last minute she had dipped one of the towels in the milk and brought that in as well. As weak as the calf was, it just might take some persuasion to start him nursing. Logan's brief glance of appreciation let her know that her years on her parents' farm hadn't been a total loss.

He signalled her to go ahead with the feeding while he continued to massage the calf to get the circulation going in his nearly frozen body. Jennifer had to force its mouth open, letting the milk-soaked rag trickle its life-giving force down its throat. At last his feeble suckings allowed her to switch to the bottle. Between the warmth of the fire, Logan's rubbing, and now the warm milk entering his stomach, the little black calf began to show signs of life, weakly butting his head forward in a pathetic effort to get more milk out of the bottle.

At this small but promising attempt, Jennifer glanced at Logan. His smile of shared triumph stopped her heartbeat for a second before it took off again at a hammering pace.

'I didn't think he'd make it,' Logan said with a dubious but happy shake of his head. 'How the coyotes missed him I'll never know.'

'I'm glad they did,' Jennifer said softly, lowering her gaze to the little black head that was now resting comfortably on her knees, his hunger satisfied. 'Will he make it now?'

'He has a good chance. We'll let him sleep here by the fire and feed him again later. How about some coffee for us?'

'Of course.' Jennifer rose quickly before the magic of his smile captured her again.

When she returned to the room with the coffee, she found Logan gone. The voices in the bedroom remonstrated her for grasping at a few minutes alone with Logan. She placed his cup on the table and curled up on the floor by the fireplace. Logan returned to find her fondling the black head of the calf that peeped out of the towels swaddling his spindly body. For the first time since Jennifer had been in his home, she knew a desire to flee from him, to escape the sudden virility that surrounded her. But she merely sat gazing into the flames, forcing the fragile glass nerves to deny their knowledge of his presence on the couch.

'I was just suggesting to Sheila that tomorrow afternoon would be a good time for you to take a ride around the ranch,' said Logan, breaking the silence that had begun to press down on Jennifer.

'Thank you, but I think I'll pass,' Jennifer replied in a tightly controlled voice.

'I assure you I've got a gentle horse that would suit you perfectly.' She could tell he was smiling, but she didn't turn to meet his eyes. 'Because I'd be there to make sure that she doesn't run away with you.'

'Oh, I can ride quiet well, even though I'm probably a little rusty. I just don't like the idea of leaving Sheila alone.'

'She won't be alone.' Logan said quietly. 'Dirk will be here.'

Although he spoke calmly enough, Jennifer couldn't stop herself from inspecting his face. She couldn't imagine him allowing Sheila to be with Dirk all alone, not as possessive as Logan was.

As if he could read her thoughts, he added, 'They have some things to discuss that would be better done in private.'

'Oh.' A very inadequate comment considering the fact that Sheila was undoubtedly going to tell Dirk of her decision to marry Logan. Another reason why the ring was not yet on her finger. She should have realized that her sister was too sensitive to let Dirk down so abruptly. 'In that case,' Jennifer said hesitantly, 'I'll be happy to go with you tomorrow.'

'If that's settled then I'd better get back to work.' And he was gone.

The following afternoon Logan was the perfect host. And Jennifer, after experiencing initial strangeness astride her horse, gradually relaxed and enjoyed the ride. The air was brisk and invigorating while the sun's rays cast a patchwork quilt of lightness from the partly cloudy sky. Although Logan was slightly distant, there was none of the abstractedness Jennifer had expected since Dirk was alone at the house with Logan's fiancée. He had been politely friendly, showing her the workings of the ranch, explaining, when she had questioned him about the picturesque buckrail fence, that its use was strictly utilitarian because of the few inches of sandy soil that rested on the surface of solid rock.

As they cantered back to within sight of the house, Dirk's car was just pulling away. Jennifer covertly inspected the thoughtful expression on Logan's face. She was struck by the ruggedness of his profile under the stetson hat. The virile good looks were still there along with the engaging crinkles around his eyes, but the levis, the sheepskin jacket, and the brown stetson hat had added a steely strength to his appearance. She realized with startling clarity that Logan could be incredibly ruthless in getting what he wanted.

One of the foreman's sons took their horses when they dismounted by the big barn. Logan smiled easily at Jennifer, nodding for her to walk ahead of him to the house.

Sheila's face was radiantly happy as Logan and Jennifer walked in the front door to find her comfortably settled on the plush leather sofa. Her blue eyes twinkled with exceeding brightness at Logan.

'Well?' Logan asked, an expectant lightness in his tone.

'Excuse me,' Jennifer interrupted quickly. 'I'll go and put some coffee on.'

Sheila didn't seem to notice Jennifer walking from the room. 'I didn't think it would be so easy,' she was saying to Logan. 'He didn't even blink an eye when I explained. He said he understood and if I would be happy——'

The connecting kitchen door swung shut on Sheila's words as Jennifer's stomach twisted into a knot. Poor stalwart, dependable Dirk, she thought, managing to spare a bit of pity for him rather than wasting it all on herself.

Jennifer closeted herself in the kitchen for the rest of the afternoon with the excuse of preparing supper. By the time the food was ready to be served, her head was throbbing with a violent headache at her suppressed emotions. The pinched wanness of her complexion brought an insistence from both Logan and Sheila for her to lie down and rest. Bitter tears filled her eyes at the knowledge that they were quite happy to have the evening to themselves, without her presence to hinder them.

Jennifer did doze fitfully in the darkened bedroom. The muted voices from the living room bombarded her consciousness with a thousand tiny knife wounds.

The hands of the little clock on the night stand glowed ten-forty-five when Jennifer woke again. The house seemed silent except for the steady breathing from Sheila's bed. She lay there quietly, wide awake, the headache gone while only the never-ending emptiness remained. At last, Jennifer crept slowly out of the day bed, slipped her feet into her pale green mules while shrugging on her short satin housecoat. She had only nibbled at the evening meal and right now the thought of tea and toast sounded not only filling but capable of bolstering her strength.

She tiptoed through the living room into the kitchen, flicking on only the low overhead light above the stove. As she filled the kettle with cold tap water, she wished she could steal away into the night and not have to face Logan and Sheila next morning. Absently Jennifer placed the kettle on the burner and turned the flame on beneath it, trying to decide whether it was cowardice or courage that insisted she stay. It felt all her will had been drained out of her, that even the simplest decision was more than her mind could handle.

What a petty thing, she thought with an ironic laugh as her toast popped out of the toaster, had made her run out here from Minneapolis. That embarrassing incident with Brad seemed so insignificant when compared with the destructive force of her one-sided love for Logan. The kettle whistled sharply in the silent kitchen. She choked off its scream by quickly removing it from the flame. Just as Jennifer began pouring the hot water over the tea bag in her cup, a voice spoke from the darkness.

'I thought you were asleep.'

The dim light above the stove revealed Logan standing beside the table, clad only in levis. The bareness of his chest with its vee of curly brown hair made Jennifer uncomfortably conscious of the shortness of her apple green robe and the scanty pyjamas hidden underneath. Her heart thudded so loudly she was sure Logan could hear it even from where he was standing.

'I thought ... I'd have some tea and toast.' She could hardly breathe.

'Watch what you're doing!' Logan exclaimed sharply as her hand trembled in an effort to pick up her cup, sloshing the contents over the side and on to the back of her hand. With a barely stifled cry, Jennifer released the cup.

'Are you all right? Let me see your hand,' he demanded, at her side almost before the cup touched the counter.

She tried to draw her hand away from him, but she was no match for his strength. Her whole body felt as if it was on fire as she stared into his face as he examined her hand. When he met her gaze, his breathing was nearly as ragged as hers.

'Jenny,' he whispered. His hand brushed the red-gold bangs away from her forehead, before closing convulsively behind her head. 'Jenny,' he whispered again as he drew her into his arms.

Her lips trembled captively beneath his as he slowly drew what little resistance she had out of her until she was clinging to him weakly. Her arms glided around his neck as her senses reeled under the ardency and desire of his kiss. Jennifer revelled in the touch of his naked chest against her body as he crushed her ever tighter in his embrace, as if he too wanted them to melt into oneness. She moaned softly as Logan's mouth left

176

her lips and buried itself in the creamy smoothness of her neck, sending fresh waves of passion through her.

Her mind tried to argue with her body, demanding it to stop responding to his touch. But she knew she was his to possess, that nothing mattered but the touch of his lips on hers and the feel of his hands as they roughly caressed her shoulders and back.

'Oh, Jenny,' he groaned, raining kisses on her face and lips. 'I want you. Oh, how I want you!'

She stiffened in his arms, a chill creeping through her body with deadly swiftness. How foolish you are, her heart cried. Did you think he loved you? He's engaged to your sister!

'Sheila—Logan, stop, please,' she sobbed, pushing ineffectually against his chest. 'Don't!'

'Don't fight me, Jenny Glenn,' Logan protested softly, seeking her mouth again, only to have her twist away from him.

Her hands doubled up into two fists as she began beating his chest, tears streaming in bitter humiliation down her cheeks.

'What's the matter with you?' A frown creased his forehead as he stared down at the tears and the angry fists now imprisoned in his hands. 'What have I done?'

'You let me go!' she sobbed angrily, wishing she didn't feel so small glaring up at him from beneath his chin. 'You beast, you doublecrosser!'

'Have you taken leave of your senses?' he shouted.

'Not any more I haven't!' Jenny screamed back, finally managing to free her hands from his grip. As he stepped angrily towards her, she added in a trembling voice, 'Don't you touch me! Don't you ever touch me again!'

She cringed at the black fury that clouded his face at her words. She staggered backwards against the counter as he walked menacingly forward.

'I'll touch you any damned time I please!'

His hand reached out, grasping the sleek material of her robe. She felt it tear in his hands as he pulled her to him. Then his lips were ravaging her mouth with punishing, degrading thoroughness. Her fingernails dug into his shoulders and a spark of red flowed as she dragged them across his chest. But it was as if Logan felt nothing, only the desire to possess with or without her consent. Jennifer clawed at him, her love mixed with hate. When she felt she had not the strength to draw another breath, he was flinging her from him in disgust.

'Get out of here!' His chest was rising and falling rapidly. The low menace of his voice reduced her to a sobbing, trembling nothing. Somehow she managed to stagger from the kitchen, all too conscious of the steely hardness of his eyes as he watched her leave.

'Jennifer! What are you doing?' Sheila cried, hobbling into the bedroom on her crutches to see her sister solemnly flinging clothes into the suitcase.

'What does it look as if I'm doing? I'm leaving,' she replied calmly.

'Leaving? What do you mean, leaving? Where? How?'

'How?' Jennifer glanced up at the pair of startled

blue eyes. 'I've got two feet that are going to carry me and my suitcase out that door and into the jeep. Then that jeep is going to take me to the airport, and the plane is going to fly me to Minneapolis.'

'Does Logan know this?' Sheila questioned after a horrified gasp.

'No. You can tell him if you want to. I don't need his permission to leave,' Jennifer replied sarcastically. After last night, she didn't owe him a thing. Sheila continued to stare at her in disbelief. 'I think I hear someone knocking at the door, Sheila. Why don't you go and answer it?'

Seconds later, Dirk appeared in the bedroom door.

'What's this all about, Jenny?' he demanded.

Jennifer snapped her suitcase shut before turning towards him defiantly.

'I'm leaving, that's what it's all about! Do you intend to stop me?' A sob stopped halfway up her throat. She knew she couldn't bear it if Dirk tried to stand in her way.

'This what you really want to do?' he asked quietly, walking over to stand beside her, his dark eyes taking in the eyes swollen from crying herself to sleep and the dark smudges beneath them that told him sleep had been a long time coming.

'Yes.' Her voice was lower than a whisper as her chin trembled traitorously.

'I'll drive you to the airport, then,' he said grimly.

'Dirk!' Sheila cried. 'You can't! Jennifer, you can't leave like this. What about your clothes, your things at the house?'

179

'Have them shipped to me.' Jennifer had put on her coat, handed her suitcase to Dirk, and inhaled deeply before turning towards her sister to kiss her cheek lightly. 'I'll write you and tell you all about it ... as soon as I can.'

She followed Dirk stoically out the door to his car, ignoring as best she could Sheila's confused protests. She was grateful that Dirk sensed she didn't want to talk, that she couldn't talk without breaking down. Last night, when she had finally stumbled into her bedroom, she had known that she couldn't stay, that she couldn't possibly face Logan ever again after what had happened. The only thing that was any comfort to her at all was the knowledge that he hadn't guessed she loved him, and still despite the way he'd treated her. She realized that, in Logan's opinion, she must have acted like a tease. Because there was no doubt that she had responded very openly to his first kiss. It was just when he said he wanted her, not needed or loved her, but wanted her as if she were a cheap tramp that he could have and forget. She loved him, Jennifer thought, she loved him so much, but not so much that she could allow him to use her in that way.

'What did he do to you?'

Jennifer started at his question. The silence had gone on for so long that she had only been conscious of the miles she was putting between herself and Logan. She had completely forgotten that she wasn't the only person in the car.

'I saw the bruises on your arm,' Dirk said flatly, 'so you might as well tell me what happened.'

'Please, Dirk, I don't want to talk about it,' she protested weakly, staring through the windshield at the
town spreading out before them.

'You don't have to hide the fact from me that you've
fallen in love with Logan, you know. I've been there
before, remember?'

'It was nothing.'

'If it was nothing, you wouldn't be running away.'
He manoeuvred the car slowly through the town traffic.

'It sounds too silly to put into words,' she shrugged
uneasily.

'Try me.'

'He kissed me. And then I got angry, and he got
angry. When he grabbed hold of my arm he was a little
rough. Don't tell Sheila, please,' she begged, her eyes
clouding with tears.

'Sheila? What does it matter if Sheila knows?' Dirk
glanced at her with a frown.

'She might get the wrong idea.' As Dirk continued
to eye her with that puzzled expression, Jennifer exclaimed in exasperation. 'You know very well that
Logan and Sheila are engaged. I know she told you yesterday.'

There was a stifled exclamation from Dirk as he pulled the car to a stop in front of the airport. His dark
eyes were extremely bright when he turned to stare at
her.

'And just how do you know they're engaged?'

'I'm not deaf and blind,' she retorted angrily. 'Besides, I saw Logan in the jewellery shop when he
bought the ring and I heard Sheila telling Logan yes-

terday how well you took the news.'

'You *saw* Logan buy the ring?' He stared at her thoughtfully.

'Yes,' Jennifer said in irritation. 'I don't have to have something spelled out for me in black and white.'

'I see that,' Dirk mocked. 'Well, here you are at the airport. Are you leaving or not?'

'Yes, of course.' She was startled by his sudden abruptness.

'I don't think either one of us wants any fond good-byes, so unless you need some help with the suitcase, I'll just say my "so long" here.' Dirk smiled warmly and sympathetically.

'Yes, that's fine with me, too.' Now that it was time to get out of the car, Jennifer wasn't at all sure she wanted to go. She reached over and kissed Dirk lightly on the cheek. 'I wish you the best of everything, Dirk.'

'You, too, Jenny. 'Bye.'

She waved bravely as the car pulled away. The wind whipped and whistled around her, tugging her coat and taunting her face, as if it was making fun of the tears that trembled in her eyes. Jennifer had never felt so all alone before. Resolutely, she turned to enter the airport, only to discover once inside that the only flight out of Jackson wasn't until after four that afternoon. Five hours to wait! Why hadn't she checked the schedules? In her desperate flight to get away from Logan, it had never occurred to her once to check the times of the outgoing planes.

Resigning herself to a long wait, Jennifer purchased her ticket. She wandered through the small building for half an hour before finally stopping to gaze out the window at the empty runway. She felt like the hare, running, then waiting, running and waiting, all the time the tortoise was slowly winning the race. A draught suddenly blew around her legs, and she glanced up idly to find its source. In petrified stillness, she watched Logan walk through the door and stride towards her, anger and irritation in every moment of his body.

'You didn't lose much time in clearing out, did you?' He growled when he finally stopped in front of her.

'I must have lost some or you wouldn't have caught up with me,' she replied bitterly, turning her face away from his to stare again out the window.

'Dirk called me soon after Sheila got one of the men to bring me back to the house. He told me some wild story about Sheila and me being engaged. Would you like to explain it to me?' Logan asked, making an effort to control his temper.

'Explain it?' Jennifer exclaimed incredulously. 'Good heavens, what is there to explain? I know you haven't given her the ring yet, at least I didn't see it on her finger this morning, but I know you're going to marry her.'

He scowled at her puzzledly for a minute, his eyes searching her intently.

'I'm not going to marry Sheila.' He shook his head as he spoke, a gleam appearing in his eyes. His hand disappeared into his pocket to reappear holding the black velvet box. He handed it to her.

Now it was Jennifer's turn to look puzzled. A dimple

appeared briefly in one cheek as Logan brought a cigarette to his lips and busied himself with lighting it. Hesitantly Jennifer flipped open the lid of the box. Her mouth dropped open as she stared at the brilliant jade stone surrounded by a circlet of diamonds. Her hands began to shake as Logan retrieved the box.

'I don't understand,' she mumbled, gazing bewilderedly into his mocking eyes.

'It's very simple, Jenny Glenn. Sheila is going to marry Dirk. There was never even the slightest possibility that it would be any other way,' he finished calmly, exhaling a puff of smoke to drift between them.

'But I heard the jeweller ... he called it an engagement ring,' Jennifer struggled.

'It is.'

Jennifer covered her mouth with her hand. Her mind was jumping to conclusions that couldn't possibly be true.

'Yesterday, that private conversation between Sheila and Dirk ... she said he took the news so easily,' she persisted.

'The news was that Sheila isn't going to give up managing the hotel, at least, not until they get on their feet financially,' Logan explained. 'Aren't you going to ask who the ring is for?'

'It's jade,' she said as he removed it from its box.

'Jadeite,' he corrected. At her gasp of surprise, he smiled broadly. 'There are two gems that are commonly known as jade. One is jadeite and the other is nephrite. The gem called jadeite is mined here in Wyoming. A very beautiful stone, don't you think?'

184

'My necklace?' Jennifer asked breathlessly, her eyes beginning to glow at each word.

'As I told you, it's jadeite. An exact match in colour and texture to this engagement ring.'

'Logan, who is that ring for?'

'All Taylor wives wear jade rings. I'm surprised you didn't notice my mother's. I believe, until Christmas, Mother thought the jade necklace would be my gift to Sheila,' Logan said. 'I've had an inscription engraved inside the ring,' handing the ring to Jennifer so that she could read it. Inside the wide gold band were the words 'Cedant Arma Togae'.

'What does it mean?' she asked cautiously.

'"Let Arms Yield to the Gown"—it's the state motto of Wyoming,' Logan told her. 'Except in this case, I think you are the one who must yield and stop torturing me with the no-good from Minnesota.'

'Are you really asking me to marry you? Logan, I couldn't stand it if this was all a joke,' her voice broke with a sob as she gazed into his eyes, trying to find the answer.

'I'm asking you to admit once and for all that you love me,' he said earnestly, his hands resting so lightly on her shoulders as if touching her skin would burn him. 'I want to hear you say that.'

'I love you, Logan,' she whispered. 'I love you so much I could die.'

'I was positive you did last night,' Logan smiled, drawing her firmly into his arms. 'What happened last night? One minute you were in my arms kissing me so completely that I thought you were handing me your

185

heart, and the next minute you were spitting at me like a cat!'

'I thought....' Jennifer blushed, hiding her face from his eyes, 'I thought you only wanted me. That's what you said,' she cried as he groaned and crushed her tighter against him.

'You crazy idiot! I do want you, because I love you. Because I've been crazy with love for you from the moment you stepped off that plane and into my heart. But you erected a wall so high between us that I never thought I'd cross it. It was worth it, my darling. It was worth every agonizing minute of it just to hold you like this.' He spoke concisely, lifting her chin up so that he could look into her face as she heard his words.

'Oh, Logan, I've been such a fool, haven't I?' The corners of her mouth drooped sadly. 'From the first I thought you were nothing but a playboy, then later I was sure you were in love with Sheila.'

'There's never been anyone else for me but you, my silly red-head, darling Jenny,' said Logan, kissing her so thoroughly that when he was done, there was only blissful wonder on her face. 'And very soon to be Jenny Glenn Taylor.'

Jennifer gazed at him, knowing she could never express the rapture in her heart. Instead she whispered as she raised her lips to his, 'Very, very soon.'